With Best W.

From

Eileen Rid

GW00949924

Verses of my Life

By

Eileen Ridgers

I would like to dedicate this book to my late husband Jack, and all my family and friends. Throughout my life, they have been my inspiration and strength and feature in so many of my verses.

Contents

My Incredible Journey

Throughout my life, I have always put into verse things that happen to and around me or take my fancy. I like to paint word pictures so that other people can enjoy my experiences.

My Incredible Journey

After a visit to a friend, a Taxi was sent for,
And in no time at all, it was outside the door.

The driver gave me a smile, his face all a glow,
And asked me, just where I wanted to go.

I told him, then sat back, all nice and relaxed,
"Do you know how to get there?" was the next question he asked.

Mind you the conversation we had was quite sad,
What with his broken English and my hearing so bad.

I gathered he was saying, "No problem I will get you there,"
Secretly I was thinking, don't we make an odd pair?

"Look at your map," I said, "it will show you the way,"
At the rate we are going we will be here all day.

After a lot of map searching we got on the road at last,
Soon be home I thought, he is going quite fast.

When we reached a roundabout, it wasn't very nice,
Everyone went round once, whilst we went round twice.

As we spun round the last roundabout, I gave a sigh of relief,
But alas, that sigh quickly turned to a cry of grief.

For we had landed on the motorway, a wrong turn had been taken,
I managed not to scream, but I felt rather shaken.

We went roaring down the motorway, miles from where I should be,
The driver said, "Don't worry, I will get you home, you'll see."

But of course I was worrying, I knew we were lost,
I was also wondering how much it would cost.

My family at home was waiting for their tea,
No doubt thinking that mother's still out on a spree.

A quiet lane was where we eventually landed,
It was quite deserted and I knew we were stranded.

It was becoming quite a drama, and that's a fact,
And in my mind, I had started my Drama Queen act.

Like how much money would my kidnappers demand for my return?
It would be probably be much more than my families ever earn.

And would my kids pay it anyway, if it were a lot,
Under my collar I had started to feel very hot.

The driver got out and the word abandoned came to mind,
But I thought No! This driver is much too kind.

Because he had smiled as he walked away,
And told me not to worry, but to just stay.

I said, "I am completely in your hands,
Just let me know when the Eagle lands."

He went off to ask for directions where he could,
And I just sat there like a piece of wood.

His return was so welcome as the sun after rain,
And my fingers were crossed, as we started down the lane.

When a landmark was spotted, we were both as excited as could be,
Poor little man, he was more upset than me.

And as we finally landed, outside the door,
I was sorry to only pay him, what I had always paid before.

But he was a gentleman and said it was OK,
It was his fault, and he didn't expect me to pay.

I walked to front door, thinking this cannot have happened to me,
This sort of thing only happens on TV.

But it happens in real life now you know,
And you have had the story blow by blow.

Next time I go on a journey and undertake such a ride,
I will ensure I have specific instructions by my side.

For I never want to go to Timbuktu ever again,
Just there and back please for this old dame.

A Day to Remember

We were going to Swanage but ended up in Poole,
But that didn't bother the incredible five, we all kept our cool.

The weather was wet, the sun didn't shine,
But it didn't dampen our spirits. Oh no! They were fine.

So Wagon's Roll off we set, heading West,
With a lovely Driver, just one of the best.

We stopped for coffee, Marjorie got herself a fellow, not a moment was dull,
She only had him for a few minutes. It shows she still had the power to pull.

I was so happy on the journey, I wanted to sing and shout,
But the other four, would probably have thrown me out.

Lots of giggles went down with the Fish and Chip meal,
Laughter is all the vitamins we need, so that was ideal.

Then off we went to Poole Pottery, five big spenders on the spree,
Anyway in there we knew we would get a nice cup of tea.

And we did with Trish, who was waiting for us with a big smile,
She kindly treated us to tea and the six of us sat around and drank it in style.

We had a mother hen looking after her four chicks…Helen you were great,
We thank you for your kindness; you were such a good mate.

When we arrived home, before we said "Goodbye and so long,"
We finished the day off with a rousing happy day song.

And as I walked away, I thought of that old rhyme,
It is not where you are; it is who you are with every time.

And for me you can keep your far off places,
Just give me a few friendly faces.

Many thanks to Helen, Nancy, Rose, and Marjorie.
You really were such lovely company.

A Treasured Holiday

You dear people have listened to my verses of sadness,
Now may I share with you a verse of gladness?

It is about my holiday in Scotland, such a wonderful place,
Just to think of it, brings a smile to my face.

Up there I gazed at the beautiful scenery in awe,
I felt closer to God than ever before.

Those majestic mountains reaching up to the sky,
Gave me a feeling of strength in spite of wanting to cry.

They seemed to send out a message of peace and calm,
It was as if our dear Lord was touching my arm.

And urging me to drink in all the beauty I could see,
This I did and a lot of sadness seemed to fall from me.

As I breathed in the pure mountain air,
I felt so good; it was as if I didn't have a care.

Dear Lord I thank you for moments such as these,
How they lift my spirits and put my heart at ease.

Thank you too for all the journeys we made galore,
Each day this lovely holiday seemed to offer more and more.

In the church at Balmoral I just had to pray,
And say thank you Lord for this lovely day.

Dear friends I hope I have conveyed to you, in some small measure,
Lovely memories of a holiday that I shall always treasure.

A Trip Down Memory Lane

This takes me to when I first used make-up...oh dear!
And the end result wasn't very good I fear.

The trouble was, I didn't have any proper make up as such,
So I improvised, well I was young and didn't know much.

But I did know about the colours I needed, plus a few curls,
Would make me for sure, look like the big girls.

Red and black would make me the finest beauty in town,
But instead I ended up looking like a clown.

But in my ignorance I carried on with this plan of mine,
I was going to a party and I wanted to shine.

The red from a paper flower would give me a cupid's bow,
And the soot from the chimney would give my eyes a glow.

Oh, poor little deluded me; I must have looked a sight,
Good job my friend saw me first, and she soon put me right.

A telling off from her and I was soon put in my place,
And I ended up at the party with a well-scrubbed face.

For my sins, my parents gave me a rap on the knuckles,
And after all these years it still give me the chuckles.

My Holiday in Birmingham

I am going to Birmingham soon to see a pal,
To stay at the Hotel Splendid, owned by Keith and Val.

But before I go there is something I have to face,
They are very fussy whom they have to stay in their place.

And I do have something of a reputation,
Because of something I did, that caused a sensation.

This happened quite a long time ago,
It was in a posh Hotel, in lovely Llandudno.

I pulled the cistern off the wall, and flooded the hotel one night,
I did not think I had the strength but it happened all right.

But Keith and Val, don't let that stop you booking me in next time I ring,
Just because the Manager called me "Hotel Wrecker" doesn't mean a thing.

And I want to assure you two, that this wont happen again,
Well it couldn't could it? I am much weaker than I was then.

And I promise that in your place, I wont go to town,
I will stick to all the rules and regulations that you have laid down.

In return I will expect to have tea in bed every morning,
And I like it early, just as the day is dawning.

I also like my tea to be special, at the start of the day,
None of your Typhoo tips, my preference is for Earl Grey.

And sugar please, and stirred twice,
With a couple of biscuits, that would be nice.

So no lounging about and reading in bed,
You have a hungry guest, waiting to be fed.

I like my breakfast, promptly at eight,
Served on a warm best china plate.

Continued overleaf

Full English breakfast please, served piping hot,
With sausage and beans, I want the lot.

Think carefully what you serve me in the evening,
My delicate stomach won't stand any old thing.

If I have any other requests I will let you know when I arrive,
And please be there to help me walk up the drive.

I bet after reading all these requests,
You feel privileged, having me as a guest.

Dear Val when you have read this, don't get too sore,
It's only your poor old Mother in Law.

Birds of a Feather

The letterbox rattled, the post came through,
I thought to myself, business letters nothing new.

But one with a first class stamp took my eye,
A business letter, all neatly typed, "my oh my."

Something was different about this one all right,
I thought, open it women, or you will be here all night.

I wondered what the contents of the letter would be,
Then I put on my glasses to enable me to see.

There on the papers was a sight to behold,
A verse from John typed in letters so bold.

I had got myself into a bit of a mess,
John's verse was sent to lighten my distress.

I had told John a story, he knew of my plight,
I'd been going down to coffee morning and not getting things right.

John listened to my story with a sympathetic ear,
He had probably gone home, and shed a silent tear.

He knew how to cheer me up come what may,
And sat down to compose a verse right away.

He understood whatever happens, whatever the weather,
Poets like us, have to stick together.

John please show this to June, your lovely wife,
I bet she's never read such drivel in all her life.

It Could Only Happen to Eileen

Eileen's just moved into twenty eight,
Looking over the garden it really is great.

People are helpful and trying their best,
To make her feel welcome and fit with the rest.

They said, "Come down at four for biscuits and tea,"
No mention of paying, Eileen thought it was free.

Come and have coffee they said the next day,
Still no mention of who was to pay.

She thought this really is great, who else can I tell?
So she took along Mary and Terry as well.

She was embarrassed at the mistake she had made,
The next time she went they made sure she paid.

We called to see her and stayed for a while,
Greeted with hugs and kisses and smiles.

She said, "Please sit down but don't take offence,"
If you want coffee and biscuits it will be forty pence.

Poem to Eileen from her nephew John Hodges

My Day at Exbury Gardens.

When I knew I was going to Exbury Gardens, I was in my oil tot,
As I ordered good weather, nice and sunny, but not too hot.

And sure enough, the day dawned nice and bright,
I was so excited; I had hardly slept that night.

Yes! I know there are times, when I act like a big soft kid that is true,
But these days bring me so much pleasure, I thank god that they do.

Mary and Terry were taking me, and they picked me up on the dot,
After I had tried to ensure that there was nothing I had forgot.

I did have a full bag of something, was everything there?
But oh, I was so excited, I didn't really care.

I sunk into Terry's nice cosy car, and we were away,
I felt as if I was going on a lovely holiday.

There was music on the journey and of course I joined in with that,
The pained expression on Terry's face, told me I was probably singing flat.

Anyway we carried on regardless, he didn't throw me out,
It was to be a happy day, that's what it was all about.

After an enjoyable journey, we arrived at the gardens at last,
And right away my oohs and aahs came over thick and fast.

For I was absolutely spell bound at such a beautiful sight,
The poet that said we were nearer to God in a garden, was so right.

For the beauty of each Avenue just took my breath away,
I could only stand and stare, what a truly magical day.

I'm sorry if I am boring you, but after my little caper,
My fingers just itch to pick up a pen, and get it all down on paper.

And after thanking Mary and Terry, there was one more thing to say,
Oh, thank you Lord, for the beauty of this splendid day.

Retirement

Retirement, what a lovely lovely word,
No more jumping when the alarm clock is heard.

No more thinking, "got to get up by seven,"
Just turn over, get up around eleven.

No settling for one Weetabix, when you could have eaten two,
Then having to wait around, before you could use the loo.

No more trying to beat the rush hour mob,
And breaking your neck, for your nine to five job.

No more trying to swallow the office tea,
The only thing it ever does is make you want to pee.

No more sitting around with the office blokes,
Forcing yourself to laugh, at their b...dy awful jokes.

Retirement means swapping it all, for a life of ease,
Coming and going, just as you please.

Sauntering around in a dressing gown all day,
Or picking up a golf club and going out to play.

Then going to the local pub, to sample the booze,
How about phoning Saga, and booking a cruise.

The mind boggles; you can look at life anew,
When you sit and think, of all the things you can do.

So go on, be a devil, start a new life,
But please don't forget to include the wife.

Robbie Burns

Robbie was born In Ayrshire, under a lucky star without a doubt,
His folk were poor and plain folk, and that is what he wrote about.

Robbie loved women, and with them he spent many nights,
But he also respected them, and he fought for their rights.

Mind you Robbie was quite a laddie,
For twelve times he became a daddy.

But in between the patter of little feet,
He wrote endless verses and other songs so sweet.

His talent was so great and versatile that,
He could write a verse at the drop of a hat.

Robbie's legacy is there for all of us to enjoy,
Whatever our race, creed, whether girl or boy.

There will never be a New Year , without "Auld Lang Syne,"
It fills our heart with cheers and tears....it is without time.

And although Robbie died prematurely at thirty seven,
He is now no doubt looking down on us, from heaven.

Oh, Robbie you were so clever,
Your lovely songs and poems will stay with us forever.

That is why there will always be a Burns Night,
For Robbie you are clearly Scotland's brightest light.

The Joys of Spring

We all love the spring for a very good reason,
It really is such a magical season.

And we feel sprightly too as we step out in the air,
Ready to share in all the good things out there.

It's a time when Mother Nature does her best,
To bring everything to life, after a long winter's rest.

First, the little snowdrop pops up to say,
It wont be long now, spring is on its way.

Then Mother Nature changes winter's black and white,
To glorious colours so beautiful and bright.

We stare with amazement at the blossom on the tree,
Such an array of different colours for all of us to see.

The birds too are busy playing their part,
Building nests that are a work of art.

As we walk down the Lanes there is much to see,
Something different, and blossom on every tree.

Pussy Willows, Sticky Buds and Catkins hanging up above,
When we were children, these are the ones we used to love.

I hear the sound of baby ducklings on the village pond,
And their newborn lambs playing in a field, just beyond.

The Crocus and Primrose are in the hedge, sweet and small,
While the yellow Daffodils are standing proud and tall.

Looking at these beautiful sights, I pray and my heart sings,
Oh, Thank You Lord for all these wonderful things.

Friendships are Forever

I have a wide circle of close friends and have always felt it important to show my appreciation of their support and comradeship. It comes natural to me to do this in verse.

Friendships are Forever

In praise of Bernard, Barbara, Vic and Sue,
Terry and Mary's friends, who I feel are my friends too.

Although I say "thank you," it never seems enough for how I feel,
For my emotions are deep, and very very real.

As Vic said, you can say things in a verse you cannot say face to face,
If what you write is meant, and your heart's in the right place.

So I am trying to express my gratitude in a verse when I say,
Thank you for the kindness and warmth you send my way.

Thank you for always making me feel part if your little group,
And letting me share your Chinese meal, fish and chips or soup.

Bless you for understanding the problem of my deafness,
And your support when, with poor Jack, I was under so much stress.

These kind of gestures on your part,
Will stay forever in my heart.

Honestly I don't want to sound soppy and yucky,
But I feel privileged to know you and I am very lucky.

I hope there will be more times to enjoy your chatter and mirth,
For I think folks like you are the salt of the earth.

A Friendship Lunch In Memory Of Dorothy

In Dorothy's life, The Friendship Club played a great part,
And the people in the Club took Dorothy to their heart.

The occasion was a happy one; Dorothy would have loved that,
Starting off in the day room, where we had our usual chat.

There was dear Gladys, as busy as a bee,
Making sure everyone was served coffee or tea.

The ladies in the kitchen were also as busy as can be,
Working hard, making us a lovely lunch you see.

The tables were laid beautifully, all ready for our eats,
And we all marched in like soldiers, and sorted out our seats.

I was privileged to have lovely Eric next to my place,
While tantalising Tony and I, were sitting face to face.

Tony made me laugh, and he tended my every need,
And his rendering of the Brummie accent was awesome indeed.

But he was a good and helpful lad, and so,
We didn't mind him having a second helping of gateau.

Seeing all the smiling faces as I looked around the room,
I thought this happy atmosphere would dispel any gloom.

I gave a silent prayer, I am sure you all did the same,
For this super Club, that really lives up to its name.

The good people that make it possible, their praises I would sing,
If it wasn't for their hard work, we couldn't have this sort of thing.

Each time that we walk into the Club the feeling is such,
That we look forward to the next meeting so very much.

Saying 'Thank You' seems inadequate for how we really feel,
We do hope we show that our gratitude is real.

As we ended our very nice lunch I know we would all pray,
Thanking Marjorie, very much for this lovely day.

Ben and Trish on Their Wedding Day

And so Ben and Trish this is your lovely day,
You are being showered with good wishes in every way.

We are all so very happy to be with you on this date,
To watch you exchange vows and help you celebrate.

We want things to go right for you lovely pair,
And in Church today I mentioned that in prayer.

Dear Trish, it has made me feel good to see you happy again,
And for that I have to say a big thank you to Ben.

As your surrogate mother Ben, I have tried to do my best,
I do hope that I have managed to pass the test.

I even 'phoned the Queen Mom to ask for her advice,
And told her of the reason I wanted to look nice.

The Queen understood and then decreed,
I could go to the Palace to find what I need.

From the Royal wardrobe a gown was offered to show the Queen cared,
But what a pity that it was covered with corgi hairs!

I had to decline, how could I not,
Though I could have been sent to the Tower, or maybe shot.

But Ben and Trish, all joking apart,
The next few lines come straight from the heart.

If the good wishes of everyone here are combined,
They will add up to a marriage of the happiest kind.

And I am sure I speak for all of us when I say,
God Bless you Ben and Trish on your lovely wedding day.

Best Man and His Mate.

Look down Dear Lord from up above,
Where Peter and Janet having so much love.

Made a vow their lives to share,
Each there own, but now a pair.

To share a home, it must be said,
Is more than sharing someone's bed.

It's being around when things aren't right,
Together for each other, every night.

Gone for an hour, or even a day,
Working or playing, not too far away.

Janet's taken a vow that she would now seek,
To make it two, no three times a week (horse riding that is.)

But Peter being made of sterner stuff,
Insists that four times is not enough (accessing Internet that is.)

Living in the Wye Valley will provide the cream,
The ideal rural environment for the team.

The dogs, the cats and no doubt a stray or two,
Will ensure that they will never be blue.

To Janet I say, "He'll give you all he can,
But don't ask for too much, he's only a man."

"Treat him with care and give him a drink,
This will ensure he is always in the pink."

It's the best man's job, and this is the day,
To speak well of my friend, and here's what I'll say.

We've had lots of laughs, fun and talk,
During our business trips from Bracknell to York.

I've listened to your corny jokes, you to mine,
And all this time we've got on really fine.

You've sunk a few pints, which usually cost me a lot,
But apart from my wife Peter, you're as good a friend as I've got.

Cut to the Quick

I am feeling very bruised at the moment, and cut to the quick,
Brian had sent me, via Freda a nice big kick.

When Freda said, "Brian has asked after you,"
I thought thank you Brian, what a nice thing to do.

But when she finished the entire message, I thought I'm jotting this down,
And you are for it Brian, if I ever see you around.

But then I had another think, and although a kick is sore,
It's nothing really, and anyway isn't that what friends are for?

He's a nice lad is our Brian, as all of us here know,
He was just trying to cheer me up because I was feeling low.

Brian, you sent me a message, that's a bit out of style,
It doesn't matter, the thing is you sent one and gave me a smile.

So thank you Brian for asking after me, it is very kind,
I know what your message meant, and I will keep it in mind.

David's 60th

Didn't we all have a good time at David's party?
Everyone was so happy, gay and hearty.

All day long on us, the sun did shine,
The party was in the garden, so that was just fine.

The Monkey Puzzle Tree looked down on us from its great height,
It seemed to be saying, "This is going to be a bit of alright."

Sunshine and laughter was the order of the day,
Well, it was a special birthday, in every way.

Tables and chairs were laid out for the comfort of us all,
Special ones for the children and didn't they have a ball.

For wasn't Grandad David, looking after his little quests,
Pulling them around the garden in a Cardboard Cadillac, "only the best."

It was Wagon's Roll, nice easy paces,
You could see the joy on their little faces.

Oh, It was a grand party, no doubt about that,
Janet and her helpers must have worked out flat.

For didn't they supply us with good food galore,
And lots and lots to drink, who could ask for more.

We sang "Happy Birthday Dave" our voices rang out loud and clear,
And candles were blown out, to a friendly cheer.

The birthday cake Mother Gwen had made with such loving care,
Was cut and handed out, for all of us to share.

Gwen and I had Alan to thank for taking us from A to B,
It was a lovely day, thank you so much Janet and Dave for inviting me.

Dear Debbie

Debbie you are leaving and I wanted to shout, "Oh no you can't go,"
But that would be very silly of me, I know.

The talk of shutting you in a cupboard is an extreme measure that's true,
But it shows just how desperate we were to keep you.

Your stay with us has been short, but very sweet,
I hope it's not long before the next time we meet.

I feel very privileged to have known you; it has been a pleasure,
And we all think you are a real treasure.

Your happy caring ways endeared you to us all,
And it was always with a smile, when you answered our call.

Many thanks for all the kind things you have done,
And always being such a barrel of fun.

And so, Debbie we have to part,
You are out of our lives but still in our heart.

So cheerio from all of us here,
And God Bless you for being such a dear.

Fred. A Vicar and Friend.

Dear Fred, as the date of your leaving draws near,
I must confess to shedding a silent tear.

When you said you were leaving, I thought no don't go,
Which was very silly of me I know.

But St. Johns will not be the same, without you in the pulpit,
Because your sermons were always such a big hit.

Your lessons were always such a joy to listen to,
Your warmth and good humour always shone through.

Your kindness and understanding when I needed it, helped me no end,
To me you were not only my vicar; you were my very good friend.

So along with your other parishioners your going makes me sad,
But I feel privileged to have known you, that makes me glad.

And so onto Colchester you depart,
Out of Woodley, but still here in our heart.

May you and your family find happiness in your new home,
Remember Woodley will always love you no matter where you roam.

The Friendship Club Lunch.

Wasn't it lovely? I think you will agree,
The lovely lunch that Molly cooked, for you and me.

When I got home I grabbed the first pen I could find,
I couldn't wait to write about everyone who had been so kind.

The tables were laid, all nice and neat,
All we had to do was sit down and eat.

And that is just what we did,
After we had admired and applauded!

The decorations on the tables, with the floating candles all alight,
And the beautiful daffodils, making the room so bright.

No wonder we all had smiling faces,
As we sorted out our different places.

Tony sat at the head of the table, well away from me,
He thought that I might write about him you see!!

So I am writing to say Thank You Tony, for running too and fro,
Along with all the other helpers, whose names I do not know.

The meal was cooked to perfection, and was real yummy,
Molly knew the way to our hearts was through our tummy.

Each one of us ate everything on our plate,
It was the best way of saying "that dinner was great."

Then there followed the sweet,
That was another lovely treat.

By Anne Chapel who really did us proud,
And I want to shout your praises out loud.

Because you made all your sweets really nice,
And all of us were spoilt for choice.

To Brenda and everyone who helped, what can I say?
Thank you all so very much, for giving us such a lovely day.

Verse to Eileen

I wish that I could be like you,
And write a rhyme or two.

About the mundane happenings,
Of odds and bobs and things.

There's nothing that escapes your mind,
The merest oddity.

Will set you writing down a verse,
Of comic poetry.

But we all love to hear each week,
Of your latest escapades.

'Cos the silly things that happen to you,
Often happen in our lives too.

So keep at it Eileen and give us a laugh,
Because God means us to smile.

And I'm sure that you write on his behalf,
With your wit and amusing style.

Poem to Eileen from her friend Gwen Rhymer

George...A Hundred Today

Oh! Wasn't it lovely at George's Birthday party?
It was nice to see him so hale and hearty.

Oscar and his helpers worked so hard to make this special day,
Good and memorable in every way.

Tables and chairs were laid out just right,
And the coloured balloons were a welcome sight.

There were happy smiles on all our faces,
As Oscar settled us in all the right places.

For photographs to be taken by special crews,
Because after all a Hundredth Birthday is front-page news.

Then we all trotted over to a waiting table, nothing hasty,
To help ourselves to lovely food, that all looked tasty.

Wine and soft drinks were there in plenty,
No need for anyone's glass to stay empty.

Happy dance music was filling the air,
That soon got me out of my chair.

To join all the other ladies on the floor,
It seemed our aches and pains had gone out of the door.

And we were about to set the scenes,
For we had suddenly become the Dancing Queens.

Oscar and Sid, good sports that they are,
Also joined the Dancing Queens, everyone a star.

George got up with Glad and danced his part,
Because like Glad, he's a Londoner, bless his heart.

He also stood up straight and tall,
Giving a speech to thank us all.

The singing too came over loud and clear,
Good old songs, the ones we love to hear.

And our singing came straight from the heart,
When it came to the Cake and Happy birthday part.

And to top it all, George received a special Card to say,
The Queen wishes our George, 'Many Happy Returns of the Day.'

All in all the Party was great fun,
Put on to celebrate George's ton.

And I'm sure I speak for all of us when I say,
Thank you Oscar and your kind helpers for a wonderful day.

Hilda's Birthday

Today is the birthday of someone we all love,
Her kindness touches us all, it goes beyond and above.

If you try to return her kindness her humility is such,
She is amazed, and always says, "It is far too much."

Dear Hilda what I am saying you really must believe,
If you give out as you do, you are going to receive.

You are a very special lady; this is your special day,
And you deserve to be happy in every kind of way.

Everyone here is giving a wish, I am sure it is true,
That everything good in life should happen to you.

So Happy Birthday Hilda we all think you are great,
And I know, because I am your neighbour, friend and mate.

Jenny's Party

Didn't we have a nice time at Jenny's Party,
Everyone was so happy, gay and hearty.

Catherine picked me up; she was in good form,
Jenny welcomed us, with a smile so warm.

It was meant to be a Garden Party, but the sun forgot to shine,
But Jenny's sitting room was cosy, so that was just fine.

But we did have a peep at the garden, what a lovely sight,
So many flowers, very colourful and bright.

And that beautiful garden needed the rain that was falling fast,
We were glad the rain had arrived at last.

So we trotted back to the house, other visitors to see,
And then Jenny brought us all a nice hot cup of tea.

We sat around chatting about this and that,
And we looked at some photographs of Jenny's cat.

It was nice to listen and hear each other's views,
And try to catch up with the latest news.

Then it was time to sample the lovely food that Jenny had laid out,
So much, so nice, we were spoilt for choice, we were in doubt.

With minds made up, it was "Bon Appetite,"
We ate our savouries, and went back for sweet.

And of course that was followed, by another cup of tea,
We were being royally looked after you see.

Back to more chat, then realising with a sigh,
That the time had come for us to say goodbye.

With many thanks to Jenny, we went on our way,
Bless you Jenny and helpers for this lovely day.

And to make this lovely day complete,
We all had a bag of goodies to take away and eat.

Lunch at my Place with Freda and Gwen

Freda, Gwen and I like to give each other a little treat,
So to one another's place for lunch, that is where we meet.

We slave in the kitchen, doing jobs galore,
But we don't mind, because that what's friends are for.

After lunch, we sit around and natter,
About all the things that really matter.

We have an enormous amount of fun,
Talking about everything under the sun.

We do it quietly, we never shout,
But we do know what we are talking about.

Because all three of us are all very bright,
And we could soon put the world right.

But it's just the hassle of getting to meet,
All those others at 10, Downing Street.

Teatime, and a slight pause when I say,
"Cup of ordinary tea or do you prefer Earl Grey?"

I can't help it; yes I know it's a sin,
When I let a touch of Hyacinth Bucket creep in.

And of course there are the usual little stops,
While I put in, my never ending eye drops.

But so busy was I talking and pulling out all the stops,
I'd lost time, and got behind with all those flipping eye drops.

I'm alone now, so time to forget all those dreams and wishes,
Time to face the kitchen sink, and all those dirty dishes.

When I survey the sink, do I think Oh! Heavens above,
No, because they do the same for me, it's just a labour of love.

Ode to Betty.

I was coming down the stairs when I heard it,
It was the sound of music, and it had such a lovely lilt.

And it took me right back to my dancing days,
Dancing that had been happy in so many ways.

I had to find out who was playing the music; it was just up my street,
And I just could not stop the tapping of my feet.

Seated at the organ, was Betty. She was playing my tune,
It was a lovely slow waltz, and I was over the moon.

A few notes of that music and I was gone,
Transferred to another world, where I became a swan.

So there was I, gliding around the floor,
Oblivious of anyone who should come through the door.

I was probably in my overalls, looking like a sack,
But for a little while, I was in Satin and Lace, with a number on my back.

All I needed now was for a partner, someone like Fred Astaire,
But there was only Charlie and Slack Alice sitting quietly on a chair.

Charlie and Alice are rag dolls, a lovely boy and girl,
And Alice didn't seem to mind, when I took Charlie for a twirl.

Charlie and I became Ginger Rogers and Fred Astaire,
As we floated around the room, we were a perfect pair.

And Betty played on, choosing melodies so sweet,
What a good sport she is, giving me such a lovely treat.

Betty your playing brings all of us so much pleasure,
Thank you so much you really are a treasure.

Lunch with my Friends

We have just had our Friendship Lunch for the year 2004,
It was very enjoyable just like the years before.

There was a band of kind helpers all doing their best,
To help make this lunch a roaring success.

Then to the sweet table, Anne you did us proud,
We all want to sing your praises out loud.

So many puddings to chose from, and all so nice,
No wonder most of us went up there twice.

Tony was helping, and as always being kind and funny,
Teasing me like mad, because I'm a Brummie.

It was nice having Eric and Fred at our table, especially for me,
It enabled me to have, three chocolates you see.

For when these came round I did something not normally done,
I took two chocolates just for a bit of fun.

Then on hearing that Eric and Fred had three I thought Oh my,
If they can have three, then surely so can I.

And the saga of the chocolates went on without end,
For Joan wrapped up two more for me, making her my best friend.

Oh, it made for such a lot of happiness and fun,
We were cheeky like monkeys, when all said and done.

It was a most enjoyable occasion without a doubt,
Everyone looked so happy as we all moved out.

A lot of hard work went into giving us this treat we know that's true,
So many thanks all you kind people, God Bless every one of you.

Grizzly Bacon and the Done to Death Egg

I find that laughter is a very good way of handling most things that are thrown at me. I try not to take myself too seriously and really enjoy writing humorous (at least to me) verses.

The Sad Saga of the Grizzly Bacon and the Done to Death Egg.

"Egg and Bacon for breakfast Terry?" I gaily ask,
Thinking it would be the usual task.

"Go easy on the fat Mom, if you don't mind,"
"No problem son" I said, wanting to be kind.

"Don't forget the salmonella scare," quipped Terry, "cook the egg well,"
"Count on me son'" I said cracking the egg from the shell.

Under the grill the bacon was popped,
Into the frying pan the egg was flopped.

"Turn the egg over," said Terry, "it must be cooked a lot,"
But while turning the egg over, the bacon was forgot.

The bacon was dragged out it was all alight,
It was crisp and black not a pretty sight.

The sad remains were slapped on a plate,
And taken to son Terry, for him to ate.

"Oh! Dear," said Terry, from the table rising,
"I can't say that it looks very appetising."

He reached for the plate, nearly dropped the lot,
I had forgotten to tell him, the plate was hot.

"Oh, damn the egg scare," I said in a flurry,
And damn that silly Edwina Currie.

Bravely Terry tried to get through it,
But I could see he could hardly chew it.

"Mother," said Terry, "don't get your knickers in a twist,
Next time I am here, I will have Weetabix."

One thing is certain in future, I will eat my hat,
Before I try cooking again without any fat.

The Hotel Wrecker

This little story is absolutely true,
It is all about myself, and a certain loo.

Llandudno was the place where the incident occurred,
In a hotel, in a bedroom, that Alice and I shared.

The time was midnight, when most folk are asleep,
And I felt quite weary, as to the top floor I creep.

Into the bathroom I went my duties to carry out,
But I wasn't in long, before I let out a mighty shout.

I had only pressed the handle to flush out the loo,
When Bang! Wallop! The cistern fell off the wall, was I in a stew.

Alice came rushing in, and what a sight she saw,
The cistern tipped up into the bath, and water flooding the floor.

For poor Alice it was a very nasty surprise,
She looked at the mess, and couldn't believe her eyes.

"However did you do it?" was the question Alice asked of me,
"I have no idea," I replied, "I only went in for a pee."

I went off to seek help, with my face all red,
Hoping the Hotel Manager had not gone to bed.

The lift wasn't working, so down the stairs I raced,
There was a lot to be done, and the Manager to be faced.

He was found at last, after searching wide and far,
Having a bedtime drink, with all his mates in the bar.

"David," I said, holding my hand on my heart,
"The cistern and the wall have fallen apart."

He stared at me for a while, and then said at great length,
"This little woman doesn't know her own strength."

continued overleaf

"Don't dilly dally dear David," I replied, "Just listen to me,
For the room upstairs now, must be a veritable sea."

Recognising my concern, he came with me to the room,
Which by now was looking like a place of doom.

David put his arm around me, and told me not to fret,
For early next morning, a plumber he would get.

Another room was soon found for me and my friend Alice,
Much nicer than before, in fact it was a Palace.

Mind you to the folks reading this I would say,
"If ever you want a better room, this really isn't the way."

Alice and I went through a lot before the night was ended,
Pulling cisterns off the wall, is not be recommended.

David told me that this had never been done before,
Should I take this as an achievement? I really am not sure.

Terry's Little Panic Attack

This little story is very very true,
It starts with three people being in the loo.

Three different toilets, but in the same house,
Everywhere was a quiet as a mouse.

The three people, Terry, Mary and Mother,
Did not know the whereabouts of each other.

Mother emerged from the toilet on the first floor,
Followed by Terry who opened the ground loo door.

Now where was Mary, Terry wanted to know,
And he called out " Mary," with a voice soft and low.

From somewhere, from Mary a very plaintive response,
And suddenly Terry's mood changed at once.

It sounded as if Mary, was in trouble you see,
Not calling out that she was having a pee.

But in Terry's mind, his Mary was in distress,
Lying somewhere, bruised, battered and in a mess.

He ran backwards and forwards like a scolded cat,
His object was to find Mary, and that's that.

Although sounds were heard, of Mary there was no sign,
So panic stations, SOS, dial nine, nine, nine.

The suddenly Mary was on the landing grinning from ear to ear,
Not knowing Terry's awful fear.

The relief on Terry's face, was a joy to behold,
She had turned up safe, his very own pot of gold.

But after all the giggling, one thing crossed my mind,
A love such as that is hard to find.

After this I think there is one thing we should do,
Tell the other person, when you are going to the loo.

The Shaggy Dog Band

This verse is dedicated to the Shaggy Dogs, a gallant band of men,
They have been going since – I don't know when.

Oh yes, it is their fifteenth year to be exact,
The pride of Pype Hayes Golf Club and that's a fact.

And twice a week they all play together,
Whatever their handicaps in all kinds of weather.

They may be sixty to eighty plus,
But that does not matter a tinker's cuss.

They still have plenty of get up and go,
Their hearts in the game they put up a good show.

Some have to use walking sticks to help on the rounds,
The courage of these Shaggies knows no bounds.

The 'rich' show off with their power caddies,
But most push trolleys, some even carry... poor, poor laddies.

They may be thin on top and minus a few teeth,
But by gum you should see their drives up the eighteenth.

Some get up at the early hour of four,
To book for nine is dedication galore.

For it is healthy, relaxing and just grand,
Playing a game of golf on God's pleasant land.

As they push their trolleys off the last green,
The looks on their faces show what a pleasure it's been.

The gallant losers pay for the tea,
But not before that have had the much needed pee.

Then they gather in the clubhouse, mate to mate,
I want to shout, "Well done Shaggies, I think you're great."

From One Old Bag to Another

Looking out of my window, there are lots of things to see,
But what catches my eye is a plastic bag that is hanging from a tree.

When I draw my curtains, in dawn's early light,
I see this plastic bag, and it is not a pretty sight.

I say to myself, I am not looking at you any more,
You are giving me a headache, and making my eyes feel sore.

And if you had to go and get stuck up a tree,
Why did you have to choose one opposite me?

Stop flapping about there in some sort of play,
Do you know that you are scaring the birds away?

Just because we have had a few blustery days,
Is there any need to be showing off in so many ways?

There you are dancing around like mad,
The day you fall to the ground I will be very glad.

You must enjoy being blown about in the breeze,
But enough is enough, so come down now please.

Or are you planning to stay up there forever?
If you think I am sending for the fire brigade the answer is "no never."

A standoff has developed; we have a sort of stalemate,
As if I have not got enough on my plate.

It has been up there so long, it seems to have become part of the scenery,
But when I draw my curtains the bag seems to be waving hello to me.

So a thought has just come to mind, when that bag hits the ground,
I think I am going to miss not having it around.

It is funny how we can get accustomed to things,
I have got used to it flapping about as if it had wings.

Oh dear, I know I am a soft old thing, I have always had that tag,
But I never thought I would get sentimental over a little plastic bag!!

A Cry for Help.

I'm a plastic bag; get me out of here,
Away from the big birds, they're the ones I fear.

I was never meant to be a permanent fixture,
I am not the right colour or the right texture.

But a playful wind thought it would help the scenery,
If I got stuck in a tree, amongst all the greenery.

All the summer I have been protected by leaves that surrounded me,
But come the fall, I will then be exposed for all to see.

I hope those leaves take me with them, when they hit the ground,
When those birds start pecking. I don't wont to be around.

At least the Squirrels don't see me as a threat,
They just take one look and then run away and forget.

But I've been swinging on this tree far too long,
I feel out of place, I feel it's all wrong.

I hope I will be leaving Dyers Court long before the residents do,
I want to be recycled, and made into something new.

So I'm calling out to someone who is living very near,
"I'm a plastic bag; please get me out of here."

The Bird's Revenge!

It was early morning, the day had hardly began,
When I had a visit from Spick and Span, the Window Cleaning Man.

When he had finished, the windows were shining bright,
And you know that is always a very welcome sight.

Feeling pleased with my windows, I was looking out, admiring the view,
When a large bird passing by, thought he would give me something to do.

So bang, splash, wallop, he left his special calling card,
All over my clean window. Not to scream, I found very hard.

How to clean it all off was the next thing on my mind,
How could that bird be so unkind?

With my short arms trying to reach around the window I found it so hard,
And why me? Why did I have to have that bird's calling card?

I need someone with long arms, and then it would be a case,
Of wiping the smile off that bird's face.

But do you know, as that bird flew away, I am sure I heard him shout,
"Here you are then I'm sure this will give you something to write about!"

"Because you have been writing about a certain paper bag,
We birds don't like that paper bag in our tree and tails will wag."

"So think of my special calling card as a gentle hint,
We don't want to see that paper bag put into print."

We want it in the bin where it belongs,
Not flapping about, spoiling our songs.

A Cold Afternoon

It was Sunday, I had been to Church and I got home not a moment too soon,
For I had planned to spend a pleasant peaceful afternoon.

But first I had to do, a little job it wouldn't take long,
But somehow or another it all went wrong.

The little job was defrosting the fridge; it turned out to be a pain,
I waited and waited for it to defrost, but it was all in vain.

Of course it helps if you switch off first, that's what should be done,
I had switched something off, but it happened to be the wrong one.

I can't believe that I would do a silly thing like this,
The fault was staring at me now, how could I miss.

And my face was getting as red as could be,
As I went to get Jan to see if she could help me.

And poor Jan is always as busy as a bee,
She shouldn't have to be bothered with the likes of me.

And anyway I think she had a problem of her own,
Because when I got to the office I heard a very loud moan.

I don't know exactly what had just occurred,
But I was in time to save Jan from using a rude word.

Jan came to help, but of course she couldn't do much,
How could she, the fridge was waiting for the right touch.

And as you might guess I felt a bit of a twit,
But at least we did manage to get a good laugh out of it.

A Comedy of Errors.

A comedy of errors was started by me,
Thinking I was going down to the lamb lunch you see.

I should have got my facts right before I called out,
Then Oscar would have known what I was talking about.

Hearing me call out for mint sauce, Oscar came over to put me right,
He would know what meat it was at first sight.

"That is not lamb," he said, "that is roast pork on your plate,"
"Yes of course it is," I replied, "that's great."

Wasn't that kind of Oscar to point it out?
He knew what he was talking about.

I sat back waiting for the apple sauce that never came,
That is when we had error number two, oh what a shame.

From beyond, a voice called out, it was Janet in the kitchen,
"You are both wrong," she said, "It is not lamb or pork, it's roast chicken."

There was silence all around, but not for long,
How could Oscar and I have got it so wrong?

"Excuse Me, Are You The Lady from Birmingham?"

This is a question I am being asked day after day,
I would like to tell you about it if I may.

This question is becoming music to my ear,
Making me feel happy, and full of good cheer.

So I had to write a verse about it, like I always do,
And everything about it is to do with you.

It is about that verse I wrote thanking you all,
Getting it published in the Outlook, making me feel nine foot tall.

When I am asked the question, I know my verse has been read,
And I feel humbled, by all the nice things that are said.

I have a little joke with myself, saying, "fame at last,"
It's spreading all around Woodley very very fast.

This has made me love Woodley, more and more,
Because I have never had this happen to me before.

So, from now on, when that question is asked of me,
I will reply, "Yes, but I am also proud to be a lady from Woodley."

You all have a sense of humour, that is very true,
That is why it's so good to share my verses with you.

Old Droopy Draws.

Why did Eileen's knickers drop down, not a pretty sight,
Because silly me had not pulled them up right.

Where did this awful occurrence take place?
In the shopping precinct: think of all the crowds I had to face.

Worst of all I was with Simon and Mel,
What embarrassing news I had to tell.

Simon walked on; goodness knows what was in his mind,
But no words of reproach…he is far too kind.

Mel stayed with me I knew that she would,
While I slipped out of the things as quickly as I could.

Stuffing them in my pocket, I walked on with my head held high,
Giggling with Mel, when I really wanted to cry.

Because Simon and Mel I am sure that you knew,
It was the last thing I wanted to happen when I'm with you.

But alas! These sort of things are always happening to me,
Because I have to have things to write about you see.

But you are good sports; you saw the funny side I know,
And it's one more memory to take with you, when you go.

Ethel's Squeaky Boots.

There has been a nasty squeak following Ethel about,
It was getting on her nerves, until she wanted to shout.

The squeak was heard long before Ethel came into view,
It was to let everyone know that Ethel's boots were brand new.

In desperation she knew she would have to get the squeak reported,
So an appointment at the Hospital was made, for them to get it sorted.

Off went Ethel to the Hospital to have the offending squeak removed,
She loved those boots clearly, but they had to be silenced and soothed.

I believe the operation was quite painless; all it needed was one man,
Then Ethel's boots were returned, looking very spick and span.

Ethel returned home wearing her squeak less boots,
And the squeak is now down one of our rubbish chutes.

Now Ethel has got back her sanity and poise,
Now that she has got rid of that squeaky noise.

But wait, Ethel has just given me some disturbing news,
Which may unfortunately mean the return of her blues.

The rubbish chute must have been very weak,
Because it never did get rid of that nasty little squeak.

And the nerve of it, it doesn't give a hoot,
It's back in Dyers Court, and back in Ethel's boot.

But it wont be settled in there for long,
Because this sort of thing isn't allowed, it's all wrong.

Nancy Sinatra said, "These boots were made for walking,"
But she didn't mention anything about talking.

But dear Ethel don't despair,
All they need is another good repair.

And for all the trouble the squeak has created,
You will be able get the little sod exterminated.

Then your boots will become like slippers, all nice and content,
And you will be able to wear them as they were meant.

52

On the Gravy Boat

We filed into the dining room our dinners there to eat,
I was feeling very calm as I took my seat.

But all that was going to change quite soon,
And I would definitely be singing a different tune.

The dinner came in and it looked just great,
Boy was I going to enjoy what was on my plate.

The gravy boat stood there in pride of place,
And I got ready to stuff my face.

I picked up the gravy meaning just to have my share,
Then I went mad and tipped it up as if I didn't care.

In the excitement of the moment I had quite forget,
Too late I realised I had scoffed the lot.

Terry looked his look, his gaze didn't falter,
I knew then I'd done something I hadn't oughter.

If looks could kill I'd be quite dead,
I just sat there as if I had been turned to lead.

I learned something then and I knew its quite true,
He just adores gravy, and I never knew.

Terry, I never knew you loved gravy that much you see,
I thought that jug of gravy was just for me.

Quickly, I knew that a good excuse was needed,
But it did no good no matter how much I pleaded.

I apologised profusely, but to no avail,
He wasn't going to listen to my kind of tale.

In his eyes a sin had been committed and that was it,
He wasn't going to listen to my kind of sh..!

There had to be an investigation into this kind of deed,
But one hour's interrogation was a thing I didn't need.

continued overleaf

He looked at me with his menacing stare,
And I took a stance to show I didn't care.

I just sat there and felt I was cursed,
And I steeled myself to expect the worst.

Mary was wise she didn't say owt,
But I am going to rue the day I tipped that gravy out.

And I have probably spoiled my chances of ever coming again,
Because I caused my lovely son, so much pain.

Forgive me Terry, and I swear by all the stars above,
Never again to pinch the gravy, that you love.

But if you don't, I'll run away and join the Navy,
And then I will tell you to stuff the bloody gravy!

Here I Go Again.

Someone should have helped me with my suitcase,
Was my thought, as I pulled it down, and it smacked me in the face.

It is no good being clumsy without showing it I said to myself,
As I knocked a table over, and smashed a glass shelf.

That was the start of my trip to Birmingham a bit of a mess,
But once there I was overwhelmed with love and such kindness.

I rushed around Birmingham like a scalded cat,
Doing a bit of this and a lot of that.

But getting into Taxis, I found I was very wary,
Remembering what happened last time, because that was so scary.

But all in all a good time was had,
It went off without a hitch, and for that I was glad.

It was back to Woodley next day for a hospital appointment I had to keep,
That meant tossing and turning all that night and getting no sleep.

I got up very early next morning, so I wouldn't be late,
But on arriving at the Hospital, oh, stupid woman I had got the wrong date.

Muttering apologies, I wanted to sink through the floor there and then,
Looking at the Gentleman, I thought here goes, Calamity Jane rides again.

Mr. Palmer was the name of the gentleman, who stood by my side,
Being a gentleman, he just smiled, and took it all in his stride.

When these things happen I could scream and shout,
Instead I reach for my pen; it is something else to write about.

Just Desserts

Walking home from school, I was as proud as punch,
I had made a rice pudding; we were having it for lunch.

But up came the school bully, with a grin on her face,
I could see I was going to be put firmly in my place.

She thought I was showing off, I probably was,
And she was going to let me know who was the boss.

The cover came off my rice pudding, it happened in a minute,
And she proceeded to stick her dirty hand right in it.

Oh! I was so mad; I don't remember what was said,
I only know that I turned that dish upside down on her head.

Then I ran, like the wind, you couldn't see me for dust,
Because I had to get away, that was a must.

I had to get back home, where they were waiting patiently,
For a lunch of rice pud that was supposed to come from me.

They weren't very sympathetic and there was stamping of feet,
And loud cries of "what are we going to eat?"

Mother was none too pleased either, as she angrily said,
"What is my favourite dish doing on someone else's head?"

I tried to wriggle out of going back to school,
But mother was having none of it, she was nobody's fool.

So back to school I went, to be punished for the thing I had done,
They would not think of it just as a bit of fun.

The teachers and the mothers went into a huddle,
And did their best to sort out our muddle.

The error of our ways was pointed out to us,
Tearfully, we both shook hands, no more fuss.

A happy conclusion, all was well in the end,
The school lost a bully and I found a friend.

My Strange Bedfellow.

I was having an extremely restless night,
And I had a queer feeling that things weren't quite right.

Although the night was warm, I felt cold to the bone,
There was this feeling, that I was not all alone.

As I switched on the bedroom light, my eyes grew wider,
For there lying on my bed, was a whopping great spider.

What to do? Should I ring the bell, raise an alarm,
But perhaps this intruder meant me no harm.

Up and down the bed he crazily ran,
Enjoying a game of 'catch me if you can.'

At two in the morning, I'm not feeling my best,
And could have killed this spider, for disturbing my rest.

But I caught him in my hanky, quite tenderly, not rough,
I didn't want to hurt him, but I had had more than enough.

Before he was released, to this spider I had something to say,
"If we have to keep on meeting, could we make it in the day?"

"For aren't you the spider I met on the garden path,
And didn't I find you in the bathroom, using my bath?"

Now spiders are all right in their place,
But I don't want them squatting on my pillowcase.

So Mr. Spider let me make one thing quite clear,
Please! Keep away from me; I don't want you near.

And if ever I want someone to share my bed,
I have got Roger the Rabbit or Long Legged Ted.

My Unwelcome Visitors

I have just got off my knees and I feel exhausted,
A problem had arose, and I had to get it sorted.

Some cheeky little invaders thought they would take over my place,
They even run up my arm and onto my face.

I have been chasing after this little lot the entire morn,
And the admiration I had for them, has turned to scorn.

How dare they think my cupboard and bedroom is a place they should be,
But I am armed with a can of Nippon, and now we shall see.

There have been other times, when they have started me itching,
Times when they have run amok, in and around my kitchen.

But I have a stern message for you King Ant,
Get your colonies back to moving that Rubber Tree Plant.

I must also warn you that Nippon kills,
So go somewhere else to build your silly little hills.

Because I have much better things to do,
Than to run around all day, chasing after you.

Poets Must Stick Together

Tired of standing in Xmas queues,
I got a touch of the winter blues.

So I was feeling a little flat,
As I picked up a letter off the mat.

I opened it up, with little enthusiasm,
It's just an advert, everyone has them?

But how delighted I was to find,
The letter was of a different kind.

And as I read it, muttering, "Well I never,"
Illustrated too! John how very clever.

The letter was from John and June you see,
Telling me of the times they had thought of me.

Mind you the times were inappropriate I think,
Not much glamour at the kitchen sink.

Now empty bottles of Gin and Sherry,
And that sounds a trifle more merry.

How about when you were stuffing the bird,
Oh No! I won't say another word.

But John and June, joking apart,
I did think of you, cross my heart.

And all the folks in Reading that I hold so dear,
Here's wishing you all, "A very happy New Year."

And I'll see you soon, whatever the weather,
Because we poets have to stick together.

Calamity Jane

Sorting through my verses I had a trip down memory lane,
And I came to the conclusion, that I was a sort of Calamity Jane.

Who else would have chosen a taxi that got lost on a motorway,
Which turned a very short journey, into a very very long day.

And while staying in a posh hotel, who else would pull a cistern off the wall,
It would be understandable if I weighed twenty stone and was six feet tall.

Why oh why did I have to have a spider nestling in my bed,
I didn't need it, I already had long legged Ted.

And even the manager said that he felt quite sure,
That this sort of thing had never happened before.

And did I have to get invaded by an army of ants,
Building hills in my cupboard, and getting into my pants.

A visit to the dentist, is an everyday affair,
Not for me though, when I go, I come out with blood dripping everywhere.

And when the family sat down to dinner, please take note,
Which member of the family got her finger stuck in the gravy boat?

Which meant that I had lots of gravy, which I didn't need,
But to the family, it must have looked like sheer greed.

And why did I have to wait until I had company,
Before finding out that I had lost my front door key?

So a sort of Calamity Jane I think I definitely can claim,
As in most cases it is certainly me to blame.

Still providing I come out of the problems with a smile,
I will continue to carry them all off with a laissez-faire style!

As befits my status as a mature great grandmother,
Calm, experienced and able to handle anything without bother.

The Biscuit Saga.

There was a sale on at our Church, and things were going for a song,
Wanting to give support, Freda and I thought we would go along.

When we got there, we strode, boldly through the door,
A couple of big spenders, the sort of customers they were looking for.

After viewing everything we emerged with a couple of books and a plant pot,
Which left us sorely in need of a drink, as we were feeling quite hot.

So it was to the refreshment bar, that we made a beeline,
Freda said "I don't want a biscuit, so you can have mine."

I felt pleased that instead of one biscuit I now had two,
One was a Garibaldi, and for me, that was something new.

It sounded like an Italian Designer; I was intrigued by the name,
But the shape of the biscuit was far from perfect, wasn't that a shame?

It was very misshapen without a doubt,
And to my mind, it should have been thrown out.

And Brenda's Fred, who was standing near,
Also pointed it out, in a voice loud and clear.

So I said to myself, a designer biscuit, this one aint,
Then I shouted for the manager, because I wanted to make a complaint.

But it seemed half a dozen of people were already there,
And they fixed me then and there with a steely stare.

I noticed that they were all much bigger then me,
So I sat down very quietly to drink my tea.

I bit into the Garibaldi and I found it very tasty,
I thought perhaps I was being just a little bit hasty.

continued overleaf

Then looking at my shortcake biscuit, I thought I don't want you,
I'm going to ask if I can have an exchange, which is what I'll do.

I will go up to the counter, and I'll smile very sweetly,
And say, "please may I exchange this short cake for a Garibaldi?"

Egged on by Freda, whom I knew was enjoying the scene,
I nearly did, and then I thought, oh, don't be so mean.

These kind ladies have worked hard, and done a good job too,
And they don't want to be bothering with the likes of you?

But do you know I can't let this drop, it is playing on my mind,
I keep feeling I have got to make a complaint of some kind.

So there's a question I would like to ask all of you,
And I want your answers to be very true.

If I write a rude letter to the biscuit baker,
Do you think that folks will think I am a troublemaker?

The Day That I Became a Dracula Look Alike.

This is quite a sad little story, so hankies ready please,
It also becomes very gory, so put yourself at ease.

The dentist's chair is where this awful saga started,
It is, where old roots and I had to be parted.

Out of my gums, these roots had to be dug,
So it was going to take more than just a tug.

Things happened in that chair, that I don't like to think about,
I did a lot of squirming, but I managed not to shout.

When I was finally released, I was just a nervous wreck,
It was as if a hole had been dug, right into my neck.

As I dragged myself from the chair I found I couldn't walk,
But the biggest shock was to come, I found I couldn't talk.

Now I know my gums, they would have to sew,
But if they sew my lips, that would be quite a blow.

For the art of conversation is something that I enjoy,
And I didn't want it spoiled, by a sadistic dentist guy.

On a pad I had to bite to stem the flowing blood,
This I know I had to do, or we would have had a flood.

I happened to glance in a mirror, and the reflection was such,
That I looked like Dracula, after he'd had a drop too much!

The Hidden Pies

Dear John and June I have an apology to make,
When you came to me, I am sorry there was no cake.

But because of short notice, you had to take pot luck,
I had to think what to give; you don't go for any kind of muck.

So what treats did I have to put before your eyes,
I had a Jaffa Orange, a Kit Kat, and a box of mince pies.

When you read this you will get in a bit of a state,
Because you did not have mince pies on your plate.

The truth is, and I am sorry to say,
The pies had been put in a tin and hidden away.

It was a case of out of sight, out of mind,
I really didn't mean to be unkind.

And of course I remembered them when you had gone,
I was so upset, I just could not bring myself to eat one.

But next day when Terry came to call,
He didn't let this story bother him at all.

"Cheers John and June," he said as he took them all away,
But I am sure things will be better for you another day.

Because your company is so welcome I am sure you will see,
You will get more than a Jaffa, a Kit Kat and a nice cup of tea.

The Sensational Saga of Mary's Soggy Kitchen

It was six-o-clock in the morning, when Terry did awake,
He toddled into the kitchen, to be confronted with a lake.

The look on his face, must have been a sight to behold,
As he surveyed all that water, so icy, so cold.

For the truth to sink in, took a minute, or more,
That the fridge was defrosting, all over the floor.

It was a dilemma for Terry, and that is very true,
For he was up early and at a loss, "what to do?"

The answer to Terry's dilemma was sleeping peacefully in her bed,
But to wake Mary at six in the morning was something he would dread.

Not that Mary is fearsome in the morning, I really must add,
But she is not that sweet either, and it frightened the poor lad.

So manfully he set about cleaning it up, on his own,
And grabbing a mop, went into the task all alone.

Then down came mother, who took over the job,
"Whatever, could have happened?" I said with a sob.

For at that time in the morning I am still a bit thick,
And I have to have some time, before I really start to click.

Then at the kitchen door, Mary suddenly appears,
She looked the mess over, but she shed no tears.

It was then that the mopping up really began,
What a pity the defrosting hadn't gone to plan.

Mary was upset that Terry hadn't woken her up at six,
And he realised at once, that he was in a bit of a fix.

To say that the air in the kitchen was very very blue,
Would be unkind, and it wouldn't be quite true.

continued overleaf

But it was a bit off colour, and words were exchanged,
Things were at cross-purposes, and had to be explained.

I was in the corner, could see both sides of the tiff,
But I couldn't interfere; it might have caused a riff.

Mary finished drying the kitchen, and it looked quite nice,
Until she picked up the cube tray, full of water, not ice.

And over the kitchen floor the water did pour,
Once more to drench poor Mary's floor.

There was a silence in the kitchen, not a sound to be heard,
Until Terry started laughing and Mary said a rude word.

"Be off to work," Mary stormed at Terry,
And he made a quick exit, still sounding merry.

You might think that this was the end of the saga but it was not,
For on picking up a jug of water, Mary upset the blooming lot.

Once more it was the mopping up operation to the fore,
Never before had Mary's kitchen, had such a clean floor.

This had been quite a morning; I think you will agree,
But it ended with Mary laughing, and a lovely morning for me.

Moving From Home to Home

I have moved house four times since I was 85 years old. I am told this is unusual for someone of my age, but it has nevertheless given me a wonderful opportunity to capture all the emotions and dramas in verse

Moving from Home to Home

This is my third day in Woodley, everything going from good to better,
And I just had to let you know in a letter.

Sitting in the beautiful garden eating breakfast at just turned seven,
After all the hassle, I am now relaxed, and it feels like heaven.

I will never forget my wonderful send off from you, my friends in Brum,
All the kisses, tears and good-byes, beating in my head like a drum.

Looking at all the lovely cards and flowers which I received,
My leaving left me with emotions I would never have believed.

Then to get a cake from June to celebrate the event,
I thought, "Surely all my friends are heaven sent?"

So thank you and God Bless, I'll remember your kindness forever,
And will I forget you all? The answer is, "No never."

Moving into Dyers Court.

I was more than a little apprehensive,
When to Dyers Court I went to live.

It was going to be a big step, another change,
With so much to do, and so much to arrange.

Lots of questions were rattling about in my head,
Would I like a living room, to also contain my bed?

Looking back it was stupid, the things I worried about,
For instance, if they didn't like me, would they throw me out?

Yes! My imagination does run riot a bit,
And my Tragedy Queen Act always has to come into it.

But things were very soon put to right,
When I met Steph and Jan, it was love at first sight.

Their conversation was so warm and sincere,
Straight away I knew I was going to like it here.

The residents I met down corridors, that seemed to go on for miles,
All made me feel welcome, by the warmth of their smiles.

The day of the move dawned nice and bright,
A good sign, I just knew that things would go right.

With two strapping lads to help me, like Keith and Terry,
The move should be good it could even be merry.

Then the phone rang and it was Terry saying "Hi ya,
We couldn't get the settee in, so it's gone to Sue Ryder."

I tried not to think of my beautiful settee,
Being sold at Sue Ryder's, for about fifty p.

continued overleaf

Getting my stuff in the flat, was tricky, the lads had a hard day,
But they did it, and only managed to smash one light on the way.

Then I was in, and we soon had my room tidy and neat,
And I was showing off like mad, with my brand new suite.

Mind you this suite isn't everybody's colour, a sort of shocking pink,
To my old one I had to say goodbye, after all it was the weakest link.

I was in time for the Xmas party, where I had the time of my life,
The entertainer sang to me of love, but then went and sat next to his wife.

Mary's Wedding.

There's to be a wedding at Dyers Court, and plans are being laid,
I'm so excited because I've been chosen to be the chief bridesmaid.

The blushing bride is Mary Margaret,
But we don't really know who the groom is yet.

All the men love Mary Margaret, but she hasn't said,
If the groom will be Ernie, Ken or Fred.

I hope Mary makes up her mind up soon, I want to know all that,
For I have got my eye on a beautiful red hat.

This hat is very refined and select,
It is on a charity shop shelf, waiting for me to collect.

It's an eat your heart out, Queen Mom sort of hat,
And you can't ask for anything better than that.

Steph and Jan want to be bridesmaids too but we will have to wait and see,
I don't want them trying to take the shine off me.

I don't know what Mary is wearing, and she will not say,
But you can bet it will be something to take our breath away.

Someone has to give the bride away; perhaps it will be Duggie,
And Gordon as Best Man will come along in a buggy.

An archway will be formed with trolleys and sticks,
But confetti is banned because it adheres to the bricks.

Oh, I wish I knew who the groom was going to be,
That part has started to worry me.

Someone mentioned a shotgun wedding; it came out of the blue,
But Mary has assured me that it isn't true!

Continued overleaf

Oh come on Mary which one will it be,
Ernie, Ken or Fred, you can't have all three.

Tell those fellows; it is now or never,
Sue Ryder is not going to hang onto my hat forever.

But alas, my dream of showing off is not to be,
There has been a change of plans, for a bridesmaid they do not want me.

After all my excitement, its bad news but something I have to face,
It's by popular demand and Pinky and Perky are going to take my place.

My First Christmas At Dyers

My Xmas was spent quietly, with my family, which was very nice,
But the party at Dyers Court was noisier, when I fancied myself as old spice.

So I joined in with Steph, Pam and Leslie,
In a free for all sing along, karaoke.

We thought we were the bee's knees, as we belted out each song,
And we played it real cool as we passed the mike along.

We were like the Spice Girls, sparkling and full of zest,
But there was no mistaking who old spice was, but I did my best.

Over the Xmas, I stopped swanning around in dark glasses,
And I have now joined the ordinary spectacle wearing masses.

I got very emotional when it was time to take the Xmas cards down,
I know that I am really going to miss not having them around.

Because each one meant that someone had cared about me,
It says so much more than Merry Xmas, I can feel it you see.

Even the letterbox has a joyous rattle when a Xmas card comes through,
And what a thrill, when the postman says, "madam, this parcel is for you."

How nice it is to have breakfast with cards to be opened on my plate,
Providing a new dimension to everything I ate.

I opened one from an old friend, enclosed was a lovely note,
That is when I got a lump, forming in my throat.

The next one is from someone I haven't seen in years,
I feel a damp patch on my cheek, and I know that means tears.

But they were tears of thankfulness for all the love that Xmas brings,
So much joy and happiness, that makes my heart sings.

Xmas has gone now, so may I wish all my friends here,
God's blessing, and a very Happy and Healthy New Year.

Nancy's Pride and Joy

There's a whisper going around Dyers Court and it's quite blue,
The whisper is a scooter, owned by Nancy, all shiny and new.

This scooter is going to be Nancy's best friend,
It will get her around, which will help her no end.

But we will have to look out when Nancy gets behind the wheel,
Because she goes like the clappers, she has got nerves of steel.

She is going to go far on that machine, you'll see,
We are even putting her down to enter the Grand Prix.

For Nancy is getting up and scraping off the rust,
And when she gets going we wont see her for dust.

The scooter now gives Nancy so much more scope,
To drive around with enthusiasm and hope.

But Nancy as you zigzag down the street,
Whoops! Look out for that copper on the beat.

Also beware of the monsters that lurk on the road,
They're always noisy and carry such a heavy load.

And children on bikes can be a menace to you on your scooter,
Maybe you should invest in a very loud hooter.

Obviously Nancy can now go at a much faster pace,
That is why she has such a lovely smile on her face.

We in Dyers Court hope that you and your machine will go far,
Good luck and God bless you Nancy for you are indeed a star.

Bon Appetite

This is in praise of Janet and the kitchen staff for all they do,
To get dinner ready for me and you.

We diners go trooping down stairs to take our places,
With smiles of anticipation upon our faces.

We are a happy little crowd,
We know that Janet is going to do us proud.

With the help of Sheridan who I must mention,
Because she always gives us her full attention.

Then there's Oscar and Kay, perfect waiters indeed,
They watch over us, seeing to our every need.

Being waited on makes me feel like a star,
I know how very privileged we are.

Then along comes our dinner, it is a joy to eat,
With lots of fresh vegetables and tender meat.

The sweet to follow is always tasty,
We take our time, there's nothing hasty.

Tea or coffee to finish, is waiting to be poured out,
We get our money's worth, without a doubt.

The scraping of chairs means we are leaving the table,
We are so full of good food, we are hardly able.

We call out our thanks, before we disappear,
To lunchtime staff, we all hold so dear.

This wonderful service helps us, and gives us pleasure,
We love you kitchen staff, to us you are a real treasure.

Moving out of Dyers Court.

I have a dream; I know that it's a silly dream,
But oh, if only it was part of Butcher's scheme.

And if only my reverie would become real.
How much happier, we in Dyers Court would feel.

If we knew we were going, where we wouldn't be parted,
And things would be the same, as when we started.

We have been happy in Dyers Court with what we had,
The thought of leaving it all makes us feel so sad.

Like any large family, we have got used to one another,
We would help out with little things, never any bother.

Now all of a sudden our lives will be changed,
Somewhere else to live, so much to arrange.

In Dyers Court we felt cared for and protected,
Now we are feeling like parcels, waiting to be collected.

I love my little flat, I love every door,
Now I'm having to leave, I love it twice as much as before.

Writing this down, wont do any good I know,
But I have to show, that it is really hurting so.

We will get through it, and it will be nice when we come back,
But just at this moment things are looking black.

I sound as if I am in the depths of despair,
I just wish that we weren't going anywhere.

But staying on familiar ground,
With people we know and love all around.

Like matured plants, we didn't want to be uprooted,
In Dyers Court we were blossoming, in soil that suited.

Butcher's tell us 'not to worry,' that's easier said than done,
For what is about to happen, wont be a barrel of fun.

The mind boggles; at what a large task it will be,
Will it keep us all happy? We will just have to wait and see.

The Farewell Party

Wasn't it nice, I think you would agree,
The afternoon tea, Oscar put on for you and me.

I couldn't wait to grab the first pen I could find,
To write about the people who had been so kind.

There was Oscar and his helpers all doing their best,
To make this party a rip-roaring success.

The table was laid out all nice and neat,
All we had to do was sit down and eat.

I know there was a little sadness in our heart,
Because we knew afterwards we had to part.

But there was a nice friendly atmosphere in the air,
Your speech was uplifting Oscar, it showed that you care.

The helpers were super; I want to sing their praises out loud,
"Thank you so much," you did us all proud.

Altogether the party was a real success,
So thanks again Oscar, good-bye and god bless.

Leaving Dyers Court.

We're gathered here for a farewell do, that's both happy and sad,
The joy of being with all my friends leaves me feeling glad.

But I also look around at your dear faces,
And know I will miss all of you going to different places.

Here in Dyers Court we have all seemed to band just like a family,
And I am sure that all of you see it, the same way as me.

We are hand in hand shipmates, all in the same boat,
The friendship and understanding helps keep us afloat.

But now we have this sinking feeling, because we have to part,
We have to leave Dyers Court as it needs a new heart.

But when the transplant is finished we can march back here,
To lovely new surroundings and the things we hold dear.

There will be welcome signs on all our doormats,
And we will want to show off our brand new flats.

So let us keep our spirits up while we are away,
And look forward to coming back one fine day.

Hasn't Jan been wonderful through all this, I am sure you will agree,
Working hard, not just for James Butcher, but also for you and me.

Thank You Jan, and your lovely staff, for always being there,
And showing us in so many ways, that you really care.

So until we meet again, this is a heartfelt wish from me,
That you will all find contentment wherever you may be.

P.S. When I return, will it be to find that little plastic sack,
Waving like mad, giving us all, a lovely "Welcome Back?"

D.Day and a Lovely Surprise.

At last it is D.Day, the day of departure,
The van has just left Dyers with my bits of furniture.

I looked across at the little plastic bag, and I waved it goodbye,
Isn't it funny the sort of things that make you want to cry?

I looked back at Dyers Court, of course I felt sad at leaving,
But the warm welcome at Catherine Court, prevented too much grieving.

I know I will get to like this place,
For everyone I meet has a smile on their face.

I had a lovely mother's day with flowers galore,
They were from my kids, I didn't expect anymore.

But next day, on my doorstep, was a lovely surprise,
It was a beautiful plant, I couldn't believe my eyes.

The kind sender, was being mysterious too,
For on the card it just said, "from guess who?"

It had to be someone with a sense of humour and who is very kind,
But why to me? That is, what was going on in my mind.

And so it set me thinking hard and long,
I thought I had got it, but I couldn't have been more wrong.

For it was Brian from Friendship Morning, my very good friend,
Brian my thanks to you could go on without end.

I hope through all my spluttering my gratitude comes through,
It was such a lovely surprise I just hope you knew.

And Brenda and Fred I hope you know that too,
How grateful I am for all the things that you do.

And so to all my dear friends here, may I say,
I hope you have a very happy Easter Holiday.

Settling in at Catherine Court

It is a month now that I have been living on strange ground,
And I've been learning to find my way around.

I have been walking down corridors all nice and bright,
Looking through the windows seeing a wonderful sight.

It is Mother Duck and Father Drake,
Emerging from our Garden's Lake.

They are looking just as proud as they can be,
As they show off their little ducklings for all of us to see.

And I bet those little ducklings are so very glad,
That they have no problem keeping up with Mom and Dad.

They are running around, each one a treasure,
Giving us, at Catherine Court such a lot of pleasure.

I am finding Catherine Court a very friendly place,
Everyone I meet has a smile on their face.

At first I found I could get lost quite a few times a day,
But there was always some kind person to show me the way.

I was a little apprehensive when I first came,
And my friends from Dyers Court probably felt the same.

But the warmth and friendliness that we received, helped to ease the stress,
To everyone at Catherine, from all at Dyers, thanks a million and god bless.

Change of Heart

Something unexpected, but very nice happened today,
While I was in the middle of writing a farewell verse to Kay,

A little bird whispered in my ear, "Hold your pen write no more,
Sad news is out, good news is in store."

People have a change of heart, sometimes for the better,
And this change has to be good, right down to the last letter.

Because it is not farewell Kay now, it is a different sound,
Kay is not leaving Catherine Court, she will still be around.

Oh, Kay we are so glad that you have decided not to go,
You are kind and helpful, and we would have missed you so.

It was nice for me to write this verse leaving the goodbye out,
Whilst giving three cheers, for a decision we are all pleased about.

So thank you very much for this get together Kay,
We are all so happy, that you have decided to stay.

The Passing of Dyers Court?

Passing by where Dyers Court used to be I could only stand and stare,
And wonder how things are going over there?

I am not being nosy, just curious. What is behind those boards so white?
Whatever, I bet that it is an interesting sight?

Mrs. Vivian Samuel, Dyers kindly neighbour sent all of us an update,
Also a photograph, showing Dyers in a bit of a state.

So I wondered if the noise had frightened all the wild life away,
Have they moved on like we did, or decided to stay?

Are the squirrels still there, chasing one another around?
Or have they moved on to more peaceful ground?

Is the little plastic bag, still stuck up in that tree?
And saying "I wonder where that woman is, who used to write about me?

I would like to tell the builders in there how clever I think they are,
But I will just have to stand back and admire them from afar.

Hark at me! I sound like some strutting VIP,
Instead of a wobbly ex Dyers Court person-yes that's me.

But whether our homes are cosy depends a lot on fellows like these,
And I am sure when Dyers Court is finished, we will all be so pleased.

For there will be a brand new building all modern and bright,
I bet it will be such a wonderful sight.

The Ladies on the Landing

It's always a pleasure to visit the ladies on the landing,
They invite me to sit down, they never leave me standing.

It is such a cosy corner where they sit,
They have a chat or they have a little knit.

They are such a happy little group too,
Their smiles and laughter seem to rub off on you.

If I am feeling down I know without a doubt,
The ladies on the landing will sort me out.

Now Xmas is upon us the cosy corner has really gone to town,
With Father Xmas climbing the window upside down.

There is a Xmas tree in the corner all aglow,
The Ladies on the Landing have really put on a show.

And sitting along the tinsel and holly,
Will be lovely Joan, Betty, Ivy and Molly.

These ladies helped me when I was in need,
"Thank You," for being very good friends indeed.

Moving Out

Dyers Court was razed to the ground,
And a new home for us had to be found.

To Catherine Court I made my move,
For the people there, my cares to soothe.

Right away our friendship flowed,
And a debt of gratitude to them is owed.

There will be lots of sadness in my heart,
On the day when I have to depart.

Parting is such sweet sorrow, is the Shakespeare sentiment,
And I honestly know and feel what he meant.

The sweetness is, I came to Catherine Court I got to know you,
The sorrow is in leaving, but it's something I have to do.

But I have to look on the bright side and say,
You are only up the road, not a million miles away.

I will have to be satisfied with the memories in my mind,
Of people in Catherine Court who were helpful, good and kind.

And the caring and thoughtfulness of Oscar and Kay,
As they asked each morning, "How are you today?"

Oh, and it makes me feel so glad,
When I think of the lovely parties that we had.

We didn't feel old anymore,
As we joined in dancing on the floor.

Walking down the corridors so bright was always a pleasure,
Sitting in the garden with the duck, is something I will always treasure.

And so dear friends, all of us from Dyers Court would like to say,
Cheerio, God bless and may we meet again some fine day.

And don't forget if you are passing the Chestnuts and you feel like a chat,
You will always be sure of a warm, 'welcome on the mat.'

Saying Goodbye to Catherine Court

At times I hate the word goodbye,
It makes me feel unhappy and I want to cry.

Why can't I be strong, and take it my stride,
Stop the tears from falling, and think about my pride.

Oh, no not me, I have to cry all over the place,
Regardless of the mess it makes to my face.

Love em and leave em, was never my style,
The sadness can stay with me for quite a while.

This of course is about having to leave here,
So you will understand if I shed a tear.

I should be excited going to a place that is brand new,
But I am still finding it hard to leave all of you.

I would like to take all of you with me you see,
Always wanting to do the impossible that's me.

I can't do the impossible but I will try to smile,
As I think of the lovely people who I lived with for a while.

I am sure that everyone from Dyers Court feels the same as I,
To all in Catherine Court, 'Good Health,' 'Good Luck,' 'Goodbye.'

The Chestnut Crowd.

Sometimes life deals us a nasty blow,
I've just had one, and I'm trying not to let it show.

And if there is no known cure,
All you can do is grin, bear and endure.

But that is easier said than done,
You really need to have help in the long run.

I'm lucky I have support all around me,
Because I live at The Chestnuts you see.

There are kind people here, who will assist all they can,
Whatever the problem, woman or man.

My trouble is helped if I get out of my flat,
So down to coffee morning I go and there I sat.

Soon, I get a lovely welcome from one and all,
Making me feel good and nine feet tall.

Ethel is there to provide us with coffee and tea,
And the laughter that comes with it is free.

We sit around and chat; it's a happy atmosphere,
Someone cracks a joke, and up goes a big cheer.

The second time I went down, there was the extra pleasure,
It was Betty on the organ.... she really is a treasure.

She played the old songs, we all hold so dear,
We sang along with voices hopefully loud and clear.

It gave us all a chance to reminisce,
We thank you Betty, and send you a kiss.

And I feel I want to shout this out loud,
God bless all you Chestnuts, for being such a lovely crowd.

Straight from the Heart

Like many people of my age, I have had to handle and witness many emotional ups and downs. It's never easy, but being able to put my thoughts into verse about such occasions has undoubtedly helped me cope to the best of my ability.

Straight from the Heart

Dear Mary, this is a special birthday and I can't let it go by,
Without writing you a verse, well at least I can try.

The years we have known each other adds up to quite a score,
And with every year that passes, I have learned to love you more.

Your kindness has shone like a light throughout my life,
What a blessing it was for me when Terry made you his wife.

You became a part of the family and my heart was glad,
Best of all you became the daughter that I never had.

Not only a daughter, but also a very good friend,
The list of your good deeds goes on without end.

You made Jack and I feel that you really cared,
The problems we had were halved because you always shared.

So many good things to remember together over the years,
Happy times with the family, the smiles and the tears.

Mary I could go on like this forever more,
I have so many things to thank you for.

And this comes straight from my heart, every word is true,
I feel privileged to have such a lovely daughter in law as you.

You are Not Alone in Your Chair

Dear Albert, in front of me, I have a birthday card,
I am searching for the right words, and finding it hard.

Besides saying Happy Birthday, there's a message I would like to convey,
It reflects the feelings of everyone, here with you today.

Each day as you patiently sit hour after hour in your chair,
Remember Albert, you have friends and loved ones who really care.

Today the postmen will be busy, pushing cards through your front door,
From folks sending you so much love and good wishes galore.

We all wish you well Albert in every possible way,
Not only on your birthday, but every single day.

May we raise our glasses, and drink a toast to your fortitude and say,
'Happy Birthday' Dear Albert, you deserve a lovely day.

Fortitude and Courage

Of life's troubles you have had more than your share,
And it hurts me so much, because I care.

Your courage astounds me; I don't know what to say,
I know you are going to be fine, because I pray.

How brave you have been over the years,
Managing to smile through all those tears.

My praises for you could go on without end,
I feel proud to have someone like you, as a friend.

And as a friend, I feel privileged it's true,
To have shared some of those smiles and tears with you.

When I have a pain, I moan and grumble,
I think of you, and it makes me feel very humble.

When it comes to fortitude and courage I feel small,
But you my dear Pat, you are an example to us all.

Christmas 1988

Christmas 1988 will always be a most memorable date,
It started very early, and it finished very late.

And every minute of that very special Christmas week,
Was packed with great happiness, it was quite unique.

It started when, Mary, after driving mile after mile,
Arrived to greet us, with her lovely warm smile.

Oh, Mary how can we ever thank you for all the journeys that you make,
Your kindness just chokes me, and makes my throat ache.

And Terry, don't think I don't notice all the kind things you do,
Just hold on son, and further down the verse, I will get to you.

And as we drove up to the comfort of Mary and Terry's place,
A feeling of warmth, and security rose up and lapped over my face.

And it stayed with me, all the time that I was there,
Because my mind was at rest, and I didn't have a care.

Then there was the fun, and all the continuous laughter,
That will stay in my memory, forever after.

The sheer joy of Christmas morning when off to Church I went,
To thank the Lord, for all my blessings, it was an hour well spent.

Then back to the pleasure of the giving and receiving gifts galore,
While we exchanged gifts my happiness increased more and more.

And even the tear I had to shed, because of Mary's thoughtfulness,
Was shed because of the feeling of sheer joy and happiness.

Oh, how I loved all those extra joys,
Like playing games, singing and dancing with the boys.

They also helped with the washing up, and made it a pleasurable chore,
For as we shared it, we sang till our throats were raw.

And Mary and Terry's friends played a part in all this,
Contributing, with their warmth and friendship, to my feeling of bliss.

continued overleaf

There was Vic, such a charming escort, and full of fun and pranks,
He was great entertainment, and I send my grateful thanks.

And to kind friends, Bernard, Barbara and Sue,
I had heard you were lovely people and I found that to be true.

What very pleasant walks I took with Jack,
A slow walk there, and a slow walk back.

With the weather so kind, and the air so fresh,
It made a lovely change, from mucky Bangladesh.

And meeting Nicky and Andrea was another delight,
Because, we all took to each other at first sight.

And Terry to say thank you both, I am now going to try,
Thank You for your sense of humour that lifts my spirits high.

Thank You for all the trouble you took to make us feel at ease,
Thank You for not putting us on a coach in spite of all my pleas.

God Bless you Mary and Terry for showing us that you care,
And may God send you a Happy and Healthy New Year.

A Carer's Lament

I hold a pen in my hand and from it a brave lot of words seem to flow,
But I know, and Lord you know too, that this isn't so.

I am not brave, I am so afraid of the sadness each day holds for me,
And I feel lost, in a cruel bewildering sea.

For how can I watch, someone I love going to little pieces,
To the point when the working of his poor brain just ceases.

It is hard to have fears you are trying to hide,
And feelings that everything is breaking up inside.

Oh, Lord you know how very much I care,
So if this is a cross I have to bear.

Grant me the serenity when I want to scream and shout,
And grant me tolerance when my patience runs out.

When my loved one is struggling to remember, and he's on the rack,
Please grant me the courage to hold my tears back.

This is no brave bold pen I hold in my hand today,
But a poor weak one that seems to have lost its way.

And my chin that I am supposed to hold up high,
Has dropped, more than a little, and I just want to cry.

But I will return to my brave bold pen,
Turn a new page and start over again.

And on a day when it is bright and sunny,
I will use a pen that writes happy and funny.

Please Help a Carer to Cope

I have a sadness in my life, I expect you have one too,
There are times when I feel I can't see the day through.

It seems as if I have a burden upon my shoulder,
And it just gets heavier as I grow older.

But I am supposed to be a carer, looking after someone who is ill,
So I know I must pull myself together, I can't take a pill.

I must not mope, so I pray and I hope,
That the Lord will grant me the strength to cope.

And I know he will listen to my plea,
To help me, help the one who really needs me.

I try to help myself by writing down all my blessings – and then,
I realise how lucky I am, and I read them over again and again.

My top blessing is Bert, Vi and Alan, for without the support of these three,
I just don't know where I would be.

Then there is the blessing of a 'phone call or a friendly letter,
They all give me such a lift, and make me feel much better.

And suddenly I find the world is not all gloom,
So I put on some music and dance around the room.

But I am really going to try, we will have to wait and see,
To think more about the people who are far worse off than me.

Sharing my thoughts with you lovely people has been a pleasure that's true,
So thank you for letting me read my humble verse to you.

A Very Humble Carer

A visit to Taplow Dixon I had to make,
The sights I saw there made my heart ache.

It also made me so more aware,
Of that wonderful staff, and all their care.

As they go on their daily rounds,
It seems their dedication knows no bounds.

Every one of the staff greets you with a smile on their face,
I find Taplow Dixon such a friendly warm place.

I watched their kindness as they tend to each patient's need,
And it made me as a carer, feel very humble indeed.

A feeling of such gratefulness swept over me as I stood there,
I wanted to shout, thank you dear friends for all your care.

And I think all of us carers should go down on our knees,
To thank God we have such wonderful people as these.

Handling Bereavement

My friends, I feel very privileged to be with you tonight,
And to share with you one of the little verses that I write.

I told you of my husband's illness, and how I had tried to cope,
How I had prayed to the Lord for strength, courage and hope.

May I tell you now, of my sadness that he has passed away?
He is at peace with the Lord now that is what I hope and pray.

It breaks my heart to say this, but I had to let him go,
For his illness had been long and he had suffered so.

I have to come to terms now with living on my own,
So I pray to the Lord to help me, then I don't feel so alone.

As a lot of you will know, bereavement is very hard to bear,
But we all have someone, with whom our sadness we can share.

When friends gather around you, their sympathy to show,
So much kindness chokes you, but it leaves such a warm glow.

A word of understanding, a comforting touch,
These little things at such a sad time help so very much.

It is such a blessing to know that people really do care,
And as well as your joys, your troubles too they will share.

So my dear friends and loved ones, I want to say to each of you,
Thanks for your kindness, for without it I would never have got through.

Sharing my thoughts with you lovely people has been a pleasure that's true.
So bless you all for letting me read my humble verse to you.

Terry's Big O

Dear Terry, I have a pen in my hand, but don't know what to say,
I really must think of something, because this is your big day.

I look at my writing pad, and give a big sigh,
And think this will never do I really must try.

I am running out of phrases to describe my feelings I know,
But have a go I must, for this is your Big O.

I suppose I could write how I felt the day that you were born,
Only I wouldn't want it turning out to be one big yawn.

So I will keep those feelings locked away in my heart,
Take up the pen again, and make a new start.

What I want to say Terry will come to me in a bit,
I can hear you say, "Stop fussing Mother, just get on with it."

Well Terry I feel very privileged to have the kind of son,
Who always makes the family proud, and is liked by everyone.

Over the years I have watched you mature into the great guy you are today,
Hard working, good humoured, a true professional in every way.

In your 50 years, you have achieved much to be proud of son,
You now have a rich store of experience on which to draw upon.

May that help you in your future years, and may they all be blessed,
With good health, contentment and lots and lots of happiness.

And remember Terry with every birthday you are loved more and more,
For each year you become dearer than before.

And along with your grand family and your lovely wife,
May God bless you all dear son, for this milestone in your life.

You Will Always Be In My Heart

As I write your new address in my book, I must confess to shedding a tear,
It seems so far away, and I'm wishing it were near.

As you move into 34, Avenue, De Belle Vue,
Good Health and Happiness, is what I am wishing for you.

A new home in a new country, which I am sure will prove,
To be quite an exciting and challenging move.

And moving in with you, I know there will be,
Good wishes galore, from friends, loved ones and me.

Your home may be new, but your welcome will be as of old,
Put your feet on the mantelshelf, have a warm if you're cold.

The same warmth from Perth Close will go with you too,
Helping you both to make new friends whilst living in Waterloo.

And although to me, we may seem many miles apart,
I know you will be close, for I have you here in my heart.

Terry's Graduation Day. June 20th 1992

The day of Terry's graduation, dawned nice and bright,
Everyone was happy, and everything was going right.

The family were waiting to have a shower, one after another,
But someone had turned the water off. Who else? But mother.

Not a very good start to the day, you might say,
It was just a shaky start, to a memorable day.

Terry had hired a mini bus; nineteen of us were to share,
Off we all went to Brighton, we didn't have a care.

Now Brighton is famous for a few things, I must agree,
But for me it's the place where Terry, received his degree.

We toddled around Brighton the weather had turned quite warm,
That was wonderful, for I had feared, we might have a storm.

So I had taken a pacamac with me in case of need,
Lovely Keith carried it around for me, a true gentleman indeed.

How impressed we were by the outside of the Pavilions,
All agreeing that the building of it must have cost millions.

After walking quite a distance, my feet were getting sore,
So I was relieved to hear Barbara say, she couldn't take anymore.

We found a hotel, of course the very best,
Just the place to have a drink and a much-needed rest.

But my insistence on buying a round of drinks was rather rash,
Considering I had forgotten to bring any cash.

I fumbled around in my handbag, my face getting redder by the minute,
I looked at my friends and said, "It's no good there's nothing in it."

My very good intentions, were taken in good part,
And Barbara came to my rescue, bless her kind heart.

The ceremony was a moving and emotional experience for me,
I stood there, tears running down my face, for everyone to see.

Continued overleaf

I didn't mind that, for they were tears of pride,
And that was something I didn't want to hide.

The sight of Terry in his gown, looking dignified and clever,
Is a memory that will stay in my heart forever.

A proud, proud day and I was feeling nine feet tall,
Then back to Reading, where a lovely meal awaited us all.

Terry's generosity that day was just grand,
For that alone he deserves a big hand.

Back we all went to Perth Close, where we had quite a ball,
I am sure that a good time was had by all.

Terry gave a speech of thanks, that bought a few tears,
Steve and Simon's clever sketch was applauded with cheers.

We danced and danced until the early hours of morning,
And goodnights were said in between lots of yawning.

And so this wonderful day ended, but once more I must say,
I am so very very proud of you, Terry Wilkins B.A.

In Praise of Terry on Graduation Day

Dear Terry, what a proud day this is for me,
Watching you receive your University Degree.

It is an honour you very richly deserve,
You worked hard for it with tenacity and verve.

Setting yourself a target, you had to reach a goal,
You did it by putting into it, your heart and soul.

Your list of achievements have never failed to amaze me,
Always managing to climb to the top of the tree.

You always worked hard to make a success of everything you did,
Right back to the days when you were a kid.

The Duke of Edinburgh's Award with medals of silver and gold,
The Outward Bound Course you did, so tough and so cold.

Have brave you were on that course and so thoughtful too,
You knew how much I would have worried over you.

I could go on and on, I want to applaud out loud,
When I think of the things you have done to make me so proud.

But through my pen I hope I have managed to convey,
The pride and love I feel for you on this your special day.

You have proved to be a winner, not just an also ran,
Not bad for a boy whose burning ambition was to be a dustbin man.

Silver Wedding Anniversary

For Terry and Mary's Silver Anniversary I write straight from the heart,
I have a pen in my hand, but I don't know where to start.

For this verse has to be special, for a very special pair,
It has to say how much I love them, and how very much I care.

And I have to let them know, how very happy I am to say,
Congratulations Mary and Terry, on this your lovely day.

Together you have given me so many blessings and that is very true,
I bless the day you both stood in Church and said to one another "I do."

I gained a lovely daughter, no one could wish for better,
Golden is the word for Mary, right down to the very last letter.

And Terry, no mother could be more proud of her son, than I am of you,
I am proud of everything you are, and everything you do.

Thank You both for my three grandsons, each one to me a treasure,
I can hear Terry saying, "not at all, mother it was our pleasure."

And as you both relive your memories along the way,
May God Bless You, and send you the happiest anniversary day.

For Baby Bethany

We have just had a lovely addition to our family,
A beautiful little girl and her name is Bethany.

When I held her in my arms it seemed so right,
For me it was certainly love at first sight.

And there is one thing that I am sure is true,
All the family also feel the way that I do.

Dear little girl, you are going to be everyone's pet,
Lots of love and affection is what you will get.

And Bethany, you are going to be oh so glad,
That you have chosen such a lovely Mum and Dad.

Your Nan Mary is great and Grandad Terry is quite a guy,
For them and your other Nan and Grandad, you have bought much joy.

And Aunt Helen has a playmate for you, her dear little Joe,
It will be lots of fun for us to watch you grow.

Writing things down from my heart has always given me pleasure,
But nothing more so than writing about you, our little treasure.

I will be coming to see you as often as I can,
Because i am so proud to be your loving Great Nan.

Welcome Ruby Mae

A big welcome into the family sweet Ruby Mae,
I would love to cuddle you, but you are too far away.

Mom and Dad looked so proud in the pictures that I saw,
You're a little bundle they're going to love and adore.

There will be lots of photos of you Ruby Mae,
So we can see how you are growing day after day.

I send kisses and cuddles for the three of you to share,
For although the miles divide us, you will know that I care.

Birthday Girl.

It was my birthday, and I couldn't have cared less,
But my family had different ideas, I guess.

A warm welcome awaited me when I got to their door,
And I met two lovely people I had never met before.

They were Christine and Ken, and I hoped there and then,
I would have the pleasure of meeting them again and again.

I sat reading my cards, that showed how much they cared,
Until a lovely smell of cooking pervaded the air.

Then we all trooped in and took our places,
With smiles of anticipation upon our faces.

And thanks to Mary, the meal was delicious, second to none,
And in no time at all, it was all gone.

Then we waited for the sweet, what would it be?
I never dreamt it would be something special just for me.

Mel had baked me a cake, it was much nicer than bought,
Oh, Thank you Mel for that very kind thought.

Just when I was thinking, "what a lovely day, no one could ask for more,"
There came a ringing of the bell, someone was at the door.

And in walked Keith and Val, I could not believe my eyes,
It was such a lovely birthday surprise.

Their visit was short, but very sweet,
Making my special day, perfect and complete.

And so my lovely day has come and gone,
But my grateful thanks will go on and on.

Continued overleaf

Because I am so lucky, to have such a lovely family,
Who are always there to help and support me.

With this pen and paper, I hope I have managed to convey,
Some of the things I can't always say.

Like I love each and every one of you,
Sounds corny I know, but its true.

It's also true when I say; you have given me the best birthday yet,
So many thanks to you all, for a day I shall never forget.

Christmas 2005

This Christmas has been a memory to treasure,
For haven't we had Simon and Mel to give us extra pleasure.

They left the warmth of Australia for the chill of the UK,
But the warmth of family love was wrapped around them each day.

It was lovely to have Steve, Helene, Alice and Beth with us too,
And Alice and Beth amazed us with the things they could do.

On Xmas morning the spirit of loving and giving was in the air,
As we gathered together, our gifts to share.

Each gift was picked from underneath the tree,
And opened one at a time for all to see.

There was ooh's and aah's as the package came into sight,
Each one was welcomed with squeals of delight.

At dinner we all looked happy as we took our seat,
The table looked great, full of good things to eat.

Alice and Beth wasn't Santa generous to you?
You are both kind little helpers and Santa knew.

Thank you Mary for making a meal so nice,
That everyone was filling their plates up twice.

Mary and Terry you had worked so hard. You did us proud,
And the family sang your praises out loud.

Boxing Day found us all in good voice,
As we sang lots of carols of our own choice.

With Terry conducting how could we go wrong?
His timing bought out the best in each song.

Mind you we sang out of tune now and again but we didn't care,
After all Christmas only comes once a year.

Soon Simon and Mel, we unfortunately come to the parting of the ways,
I hope you are taking with you memories of these happy days.

It's been lovely having you here, and to think of you leaving makes me sad,
But I will think of this lovely Christmas and be grateful and glad.

Dear Joe

Dear Joe, I hear that you have been ill, but now you are better,
I can't come and visit you, but I can write you a letter.

I was sad when I heard that you were in the hospital my friend,
So it's great that you are back home and on the mend.

You see Joe, you and Lina made some good friends in the UK,
We all love you both and want you to be OK.

We may be thousands of miles apart,
But there's a place for you and Lina here in my heart.

So come on Joe take care, and take it easy,
We don't like to hear of you feeling queasy.

Because don't forget, you promised to be gay and hearty,
When you come to my hundredth birthday party...o-ooh!

Mel's Mom and Dad

The time between us saying hello and goodbye has been too short for me,
I like to keep lovely people around me, you see.

Melina has done a lot of things to make me glad,
One of the nicest was getting us to meet her Mum and Dad.

Whilst you have been with us, the weather has left much to be desired,
I do hope that you haven't been too cold and too tired.

I just hope that the warmth of the feelings we have for you,
Has rubbed off and stopped you feeling too blue.

Lina and Joe, go back home with our good wishes ringing in your ear,
And although you are miles away, in our hearts you will always be near.

Getting Ready for Xmas.

I really must get on with my Xmas cards I say to myself,
As I pull a large box of cards off the shelf.

Well maybe tomorrow will be a better day,
I will have more time I hear myself say.

But putting off tomorrow is a silly thing to do,
For tomorrow never comes, we all know that is true.

Since then two weeks have gone by,
Gosh! Doesn't the time fly.

Does anyone else feel like this?
For really it is a ritual I would never miss.

For don't we all love those cards coming through the door,
And the warm feeling as you pick them up off the floor.

Because isn't it all part of Xmas and the joy of sharing?
And all the festive love and the caring.

Oh yes it can be busy and tiring I know,
But it is the Lord's Day, and we love it so.

Up to date I have about eighty cards to write,
Keep cool, calm and collected, don't take fright,

Is it the energy that you are lacking?
Go on, pick up a pen and just get cracking.

Until you have put on the last stamp,
Then you can go to bed with writer's cramp.

Goodbye Christmas

Christmas is over and I look around,
Time to take the trimmings down.

Collecting the cards up, seems to be the 'to do' thing,
I think it's called, 'pulling at the heart string.'

I have put them in a bag now, to be taken away,
I didn't want to do it, I wanted them to stay.

I can get sentimental over each card,
No wonder I find the parting so very hard.

But better get on with putting Xmas away,
The way I do it, could take all day.

Little Donkey has been put away with Red Nose Reindeer,
There they will stay for another year.

'Jingle Bells,' made way for 'Auld Lang Syne,'
Letting in the New Year and that was fine.

New Year resolutions, I wont bother to make,
I mean well at the time, but they are easy to break.

But there is one more thing I really must do,
It is to wish a Happy New Year Dear Chestnuts to you.

Simon's 30th

This is a poem about our Simon,
Who isn't simple or a pie-man.

But is instead turning thirty,
An age when most men get quite shirty.

Life has changed and life moves on,
And the best years it seems have gone.

And so to maintain the youth and vigour,
A daily work out keeps the figure.

But Simon you don't have to worry,
You've survived the years of beer and curry.

With dignity and grace intact,
The slim waistline that others lacked.

But as the years have rolled on by,
You often stop to ask me, "Why?"

Those thirty years have been so kind,
You've keep those looks and kept your mind.

And so I answer with the truth,
The reason why you've kept your youth,

The family's gene has taken hold,
It prevents us all from getting old.

But sadly nothing in life is free,
It happened to Dad and it will happen to me.

We can go through life without a care,
The downside is we lose our hair.

Simon and Mel's Wedding Day

How delighted we are that you are in the U.K,
To celebrate your lovely wedding day.

Giving the family and close friends too,
The privilege of sharing it with you.

Because for all of us, you are very dear,
And on your special day we wanted to be near.

There will be tears shed, but they will be tears of happiness,
I will have to tuck a hankie in the sleeve of my posh dress.

Simon and Mel, this is your day of all days,
We want to wish you joy not just for today, but always.

When you go back to Australia you will be missed so much,
The only consolation will be to keep in touch.

So off you sail now, across the sea of matrimony,
With our good wishes that happy your journey will always be.

Mel and Simon…Their Big Day

December the fourteenth, 2003, was very special in a way,
Because it was Simon and Mel's Wedding Day.

The day dawned nice and bright,
And everything was going just right.

Until I turned up, then there was a mishap,
As I spilled a glass of orange juice into my lap.

Everyone was kind and understood,
And the waiters mopped me up as best they could.

I just sat there feeling very damp and sticky,
And I knew that to feel smart after that was going to be tricky.

I just hoped my damp patch wouldn't show up on the photographs,
But if it did, never mind, it would get a few laughs.

But I soon forgot about looking in style,
When I saw Mel walking down the aisle.

She was indeed a vision of loveliness,
Dazzling in her beautiful gold dress.

Simon too looked so smart and debonair,
I could only stand, admire and stare.

Then the love I feel for these two welled up into my throat,
Tears came and I had to hide my face in my coat.

And I wanted to shout "Back to Australia you cannot go,"
But that was really silly of me I know.

I will have some lovely memories when you do go,
Of all your acts of kindness that helped me so.

Mel and Simon, now and again in your busy life, stop and pause,
Think of everyone who love you so, not forgetting old droopy draws.

Thanks For Your Kindness

I believe one should always say "thank you," when it is appropriate and I have found that writing a verse is a nice way to show one's appreciation.

Thanks for Your Kindness

When Bernadette invited us to her home, it was a nice surprise,
And when we saw her lovely garden we could not believe our eyes.

Rose, Kath and I stood there we didn't know what to say,
For the scene before us just took our breath away.

There were pots of beautiful flowers, glorious colours of all kind,
And the word immaculate came into my mind.

Mother Margaret had never ever prepared us for anything like this,
The invitation had been given quietly, and for this she deserves a kiss.

There were steps to a swimming pool with shrubs and trees surrounding it,
We weren't dressed for swimming, so we looked for somewhere to sit.

Bernadette, being the perfect hostess, made us as comfortable as could be,
Then indoors she went, to make a lovely cup of tea.

Along with cakes and biscuits, strawberries and cream to follow,
All this kindness brought a lump to my throat, making it hard to swallow.

Bernadette and Margaret waited on us, seeing to our every need,
Rose, Kath and I were the lucky ones, Oh, yes indeed.

It was the perfect afternoon, giving us a memory to treasure,
Thank You Bernadette and Margaret for giving us that lovely pleasure.

Giving Thanks to Friendship Morning

I love Friendship Morning; it means such a lot to me,
The atmosphere is so warm and friendly, I think you will agree.

A lot of work goes into making it the lovely Club that we know,
This verse is in praise of all the kind people who make it so.

First of all there is Brenda who comes along in her Car,
To give Gwen and I a lift. Oh, Gwen how lucky we are.

And what a lovely welcome we all get when we arrive,
By Brenda, Joan and Signey, making us feel glad that we are alive.

Then out comes Gladys, with her pleased to see you smile,
Saying, "There will be tea and coffee along in a little while."

Because Anne is in the kitchen as busy as a bee,
Making lots and lots of drinks for you, and for me.

Then there is Chris, who shows such kind care,
By bringing beautiful flowers for all of us to share.

Sometimes our weather can cause a little gloom,
But the flowers that Chris brings, soon brightens up the room.

Greeting one another again seems to give us so much pleasure,
For we all know that the gift of friendship is a thing we should treasure.

Verses from Gladys and Eric, then prayers, give us thought for the day,
While words of wisdom from Brenda, Joan and Signey, help us on our way.

But before we go, there is Tony our lovely Handy Man,
Putting things back in order, until the Room is left spick and span.

For all these kind people who dive in and help whatever the cause,
Let's show our thanks by putting our hands together, for a round of applause.

In Praise of Jan, Warden and Friend

Dear Jan, what you did the other day meant a lot to me,
Without the kindness of you and Mary, where would I be?

I want to say thanks for your kindness, but where to start?
I know it's your job, but you have such a big heart.

I want to say thanks and it's a pen I have to reach for,
The words "thank you," in writing, makes it sound just that bit more.

So to try and show how I feel down on paper it has to go,
And Jan you will understand all this I know.

You were such a good friend in my hour of need,
Having you as a friend, as well as a Warden, I feel privileged indeed.

You are always there for us, that is the sort of person I have found you to be,
So bless you Jan, for your kindness to everyone, not just me.

In Praise of Maggie and Pat.

Forget about Vidal Sassoon and Teasy Weasy, we are not into all that,
Here in Dyers Court, we have our own Hair Stylists, Maggie and Pat.

They do such wonders for all us girls,
Keeping us looking trim with waves and curls.

We all have styles to suit our own face,
We come out of the salon, without a hair out of place.

When I visit Pat she is not just a hairdresser, she is also a friend,
She understands my deafness, and that helps me no end.

Maggie and Pat are very kind and they aim to please,
Putting everyone whatever their disability, entirely at ease,

They are always ready to grant our requests,
"Blow dry madam or perhaps short back and sides will suit you best?"

To me the magic of transformation never fails,
Because Pat does wonders with my rats tails.

The men too are kept looking very smart,
And for that Maggie and Pat play a big part.

Having our hair kept clean and tidy, to us ladies it means a lot,
We are so lucky to have Maggie and Pat right here on the spot.

Clean Clothes

I love those two dogs in Emmerdale watching the washing machine,
They are so cute and cuddly it makes a lovely scene.

Here in Dyers Court, we have our own weekly soap,
With two lovely leading ladies, Pam and Leslie, who help us cope.

And this verse is a tribute to Pam and Lesley,
Who do so much washing for you and me.

And they do the very best they can,
To keep us all looking spic and span.

They wash everything from undies to socks,
No wonder we look as if we have just stepped out of a bandbox.

Looking at all that washing it is such a long list,
I marvel that they don't get their knickers in a twist.

The bags mount up in the Laundry Room to such a big pile,
But they get through it all, with good humour and a smile.

To say a big thank you to Pam and Lesley, I know every one of us is keen,
So God Bless you both, for getting our washing so clean.

Oh, and I must say, the dogs in Emmerdale, just like you, are a star,
But Pam and Lesley, you are much better looking than they are.

In Praise of the Nurses from Wokingham

Sometimes life seems to hit us below the belt,
Well! I was feeling sorry for myself and that is how I felt.

A spell in the hospital left me feeling as low as could be,
And then something nice happened to me.

A band of lovely nurses came to visit morning and night,
And it helped to put my miserable world right.

Just to see their cheerful faces,
Sent my spirits up ten paces.

They came when I really had a need,
Ministering Angels? Oh yes indeed.

Their caring kindness meant so much,
They really have that special touch.

Well they are special people without a doubt,
People we just couldn't do without.

Every morning my spirit would soar,
As I eagerly await their knock on the door.

They would bring their cheerfulness into the room,
Guaranteed to lift anyone's gloom.

Oh, you lovely nurses I hope that this verse will convey,
What it is I am trying to say.

It is my way of saying 'thank you' you see,
For all the caring kindness you showed to me.

Jack of All Trades

I know a Jack of All Trades, not a mechanic, or a builder,
She is here, right next door, my lovely friend Hilda.

She is a Mother Theresa; of that there is no doubt,
Always on the spot, helping everyone out.

If there is a stray dog or a mangy cat,
They will be found, waiting to be fed, on Hilda's mat.

She is a nanny, a nurse, a carer the lot,
If I need help she is there on the dot.

As I sit here, feeling ill, plastered up and sore,
I really thank God that I have Hilda next door.

Menu a la Court

I would like to shout Janet's praises out loud,
Because she really, really does us proud.

Everyday she cooks a very tasty dinner,
Each one she cooks is a sure winner.

I look forward to going to eat because, for me,
It is not the food, it's the great company.

Oscar and Kath make the perfect waiters, we couldn't have better,
They get everything right, to the very last letter.

We eat to the sound of music, it fills the air,
Which makes me want to dance right out of my chair.

But that is not allowed we are there to eat,
So I just tap my feet to the sound of the beat.

I am always the last to finish my food,
Nobody tells me to get a move on, they wouldn't be that rude.

Everyone is so good-natured; they don't seem to mind,
So can I thank you all for being so kind.

With Janet's good food on the table I pick up my fork and my knife,
And I say to myself this is really one of the pleasures of life.

To Janet, Oscar and Kath we say Bon Appetite,
Many thanks to you all for making our lunch such a treat.

Moonstruck

If there is a full moon tonight, it won't mean a thing to me,
But it will mean quite a lot to Marjorie.

Marjorie is our Resident Clown,
She always smiles, even when she is down.

And it is said, and this could be true,
Her smile is fixed with Super Glue.

You can always tell when she's around,
She has a laugh, like no other sound.

And that laugh is heard by me and you,
Long before Marjorie comes into view.

But be warned if you hear howling in the night,
Keep well away, keep out of sight.

Far more mad than usual, is Marjorie when it's a full moon,
She is restless as a kite, and as silly as a goon.

And the chaos that she causes, wherever she goes,
Makes you feel shivery, from your head to your toes.

She is so energetic, she wont want to sleep,
Doors will be opened; we will all want to peep.

And I will be standing, with pen and paper, to write it all down,
The antics of Dear Marjorie, our Resident Clown.

Thanks Brenda

Brenda, you're leaving, and I wanted to shout, "No, you can't go,"
But that would have been very silly of me I know.

But we all like to cling on to good things whatever,
And you and Friendship Morning were so good together.

You have to move on, but you will be missed so much,
We will miss your happy smile and your friendly touch.

Friendship Morning is something we all look forward too,
We wouldn't have that pleasure if it weren't for you.

You and Fred showed how much you care,
By picking up the disabled, and getting us there.

You transported us all from door to door,
We have such a lot to thank you for.

So as you leave, all our good wishes go with you too,
And we are left with lots of lovely memories of you.

Thanks Doctor Hamilton

Dear Dr. Hamilton, this is to try and say "Thank you," but how to start,
But whatever is written will have come straight from the heart.

Your patients really appreciate your honesty in what you say,
You put it over in such a kind and thoughtful way.

We come to you with our stomachs tied in a knot,
Your joviality relaxes us, and it helps such a lot.

Are we patients' glad that you became a Doctor? Oh you bet,
For we know at one stage, you could have become a vet.

We are amazed that being so busy helping patients as you do,
You also find the time to be a lovely father too.

Each time I visit you, makes me become more aware,
Of your dedication, and how much you care.

And your kindness to each one of us, as you tend to our need,
Makes me as a patient, feel very humble indeed.

Saying a million thanks to you, will only be a small part,
Of the deep appreciation, I feel here in my heart.

I hope some of it comes over to you, if only in small measure,
For bless you Doctor Hamilton, you really are a treasure.

A Special Letter For Freda

Dear Freda, I would like to thank you for being my friend,
Having your friendship has helped me, no end.

When we are in a noisy room and I don't hear,
Thank you for always being so near.

You put me in the picture, for there is no doubt,
With my problem, I could easily feel left out.

But that is not the case at all you see,
I am lucky, I have you sitting right next to me.

And when we are walking it is so good to know,
I can hold onto your arm as away we go.

I enjoy our conversations and the giggles in between,
We know what's what about everything, we are so keen.

We know what is wrong with the world today,
And we would soon put it right if we had our way.

Now and again we stop for refreshments, just a small break,
We enjoy the special lunch, each other likes to make.

Nothing too spectacular, just an easy meal,
It's the company that makes it, that is how I always feel.

And your company Freda is always a pleasure,
It is something that I will always treasure.

Birthday Message to Bert.

Hello Bert! I am the Dalmatian on the cover, and I'm on the ball,
With a birthday message I have to recall.

And I have one here for you,
It's from your big sister, who loves you true.

And she wants you to know on your special day,
That she thinks you are great in every way.

And she says you deserve, only the very best,
That is why she chose me, above all the rest.

She knows when it comes to dogs you can't resist us,
Better than a big posh card with all the fuss.

If I could come in the flesh, it would be better I know,
What a pity that this cannot be so.

When it comes to celebrating, you don't want it I know,
But Bert your family, they do, because they love you so.

So, "Happy Birthday," Bert and God Bless,
Enjoy your day with Bev, Brian, Alan and Ness.

Trying to Grow Old Gracefully.

I know that I am not getting any younger and that suffering from disabilities can be very debilitating. I find that I can retain a certain equilibrium by putting my feelings into verse and trying to be optimistic about most things I do.

Trying to Grow Old Gracefully.

Opening the fridge door, I had to stop and think what I was about,
Was I putting something in, or was I taking something out?

You are getting old, I said to myself with a crack in the voice,
Face up to it; accept it, because you have no choice.

I am hoping that not too much of it is showing,
But slowly and surely, my get up and go is going.

And I hope my younger friends will understand,
If my steps sometimes falter and I have an unsteady hand.

I bless all those who know that my ears today,
Have to really strain to catch the things that they say.

Growing old gracefully, I am tying hard to do that,
Struggling to keep slim and not put on any fat.

But it is much easier said than done,
Lots of hard work and not all that much fun.

Running around collecting all the devices needed for my declining years,
Managing to smile my thanks whilst secretly shedding a few tears.

I open a drawer to check on all the things I have got,
Specs, hearing aid, pension book, bus pass, I think I have the lot.

I tell myself it is not all sad, as it may seem,
Think what fun it is rubbing in anti-wrinkle cream!

And the keep fit routine is quite a giggle,
As I jump up and down then bend and wriggle.

If I manage to keep it all up, I may be too late,
To make an appearance on Cilla's blind date.

I'm off to the chiropodist now, oh aren't I so glad,
That I have it all written down on a memo pad.

The road to growing old is rough and you lose things on the way,
But one thing I would like to keep dear Lord if I may.

A sense of humour, has to be kept at all cost,
For without that, I know I would be really lost.

Keeping Your Chin Up (or Down)

On the 11th Oct I arose with the dawn,
Well! I didn't want to be late, it was my operation morn.

I have had this operation once, it was sometime in June,
So it could not be over for me, a minute too soon.

It was quite an ordeal, one I didn't want to repeat,
But it had to be, to make the operation complete.

And that is why I was up at four-thirty that morning,
I wasn't bright eyed and bushy tailed, I just couldn't stop yawning.

When I got to the hospital, my smile fell still in a frozen face,
As I walked to the theatre at a very slow pace.

I was invited to make myself comfortable at the operating table,
But with feet stuck to the ground legs like jelly, I found I wasn't able.

"Can I have someone to hold my hand please sir?" I said,
And they gave me this lovely fellow, and his name was Ted.

I held onto Ted's hand ever so tight,
It felt safe and good, and I knew I was going to be all right.

Through all the voices I heard one stand out loud and clear,
"Keep your chin down, Mrs. Ridgers, chin down Mrs. Ridgers there's a dear."

Then there was this voice again this time ending with a sigh,
"Keep your chin down Mrs. Ridgers if you want to hang on to your eye."

And being a good pupil, of course I tried,
The other alternative being I could have cried,

But thankfully it's all over, and I'm feeling much better,
My chin's not down but up again, as I can now read a letter.

And I can sit and watch tele wondering what's on next,
Because now thankfully I can again see tele-text.

Regaining ones former sight is a joy to behold,
Maybe, after all I'm not really that old!!

Mugger's Paradise

I love to write verses, for me it is a pleasant pastime,
Putting words together, trying to make them rhyme.

Writing has given me so much pleasure,
Helping to keep alive, memories that I treasure.

Writing the silly ones, has always been great fun,
Especially when I write them to Terry, my son.

But writing this one, will give me no pleasure whatsoever,
For it's about people who are vicious, but think they are clever.

It's about their victims, who are mugged every day,
And are trapped in their misery, while the muggers get away.

They are cowards, who prey on the weak and the old,
And lots get away, because of their age, so I am told.

I feel like someone crying out in a wilderness,
Trying to voice my thoughts about this awful mess.

I am pondering here trying to find words that are suitable,
Knowing full well that what I want to write is unprintable.

If you think this verse is becoming very sad,
It's because I am a victim too, and am very very mad.

I am mad to think that the bullies have put me through so much stress,
And because of them, before I go out, I have to think how to dress.

By comparison, what happened to me, does not seem to have mattered,
By the side of all the poor souls, who have been bruised and battered.

The Police have been kind; I know that they care,
I just wish those in charge, would become more aware.

And put a lot more Police back on the beat,
Then us oldies wouldn't be so afraid to walk down the street.

My Two Lovely Helpers

There were two little girls; they weren't sitting on a wall,
They were standing right beside me, waiting for my call.

One was from Hastings, Alice was her name,
Bethany came from Yorkshire, their ages about the same.

They were staying with Terry and Mary, a thing they love to do,
I was also lucky; I was there for the day too.

Now these little girls are kind as kind can be,
They knew I needed help, and they were going to be there for me.

So with one each side of my body, down the garden we went,
To admire the lovely trees and flowers, that the good lord had sent.

As we walked in the garden amongst the trees so tall,
We sang All Things Bright and Beautiful, All Creatures Great and Small.

And holding their dear little hands, the feeling was such,
I wanted to cry, I loved them so much.

I pulled myself together and we went and sat on the swing,
And the three of us laughed as we swayed, and my heart began to sing.

We went back in the house, and decided to play a card game,
I've lost my touch, but it was easy, Snap was the name.

Alice and Beth thank you for being so kind and so sweet,
All your considerate helping, made my day complete.

Because girls, you were delightful company, I couldn't have had better,
So if you like this verse, could you let me know in a letter?

And so my dear little helpers, you had to fly away,
But I do look forward to you coming back another day.

"Open Sesame"

My kitchen is a quiet place, until I want to open a tin,
Then I lose control and go into a spin.

Keep calm I say to myself, approach it from a different angle,
Whatever you do, don't get your knickers in a tangle.

So I try every gadget in the kitchen drawer,
Until I am blue in the face, and my fingers are sore.

In desperation, I look for a helper, but they are hard to find,
So I go to Barry, for he is very kind.

Barry opens the tin; I empty the contents on a plate,
My blood pressure comes down; I am in a much calmer state.

Then there's a bottle to open, I let out a sigh,
It becomes another struggle and I am ready to cry.

These things are sent to try us, so the story goes,
Well, they try my patience, and I'm afraid it shows.

But if I manage to open something, which is hardly ever,
I want to run around and shouting, "Look everyone, aren't I clever."

So the moral is, don't try to open an object if you want to stay cool,
Just wait for someone to invent a magic tool.

Or better still, a can that needs no key,
You simply say, "Open Sesame."

Shopping with Wally,

Wally the trolley stands in the hall waiting for me,
Because today we are going shopping you see.

I check to see that I have all the things I need to take,
I know from the past, the mistakes I can make.

I can write a list, well as much as I am able,
Then find that I have left it on the kitchen table.

On the list of course are all the things I really need,
Am I a stupid person? Oh yes indeed.

And I must check I have the money to pay the bill,
Don't want to find I haven't when I get to the till.

Back to Wally, who like me is sagging in places, I pull him together,
Then off we go, whatever the weather.

Waitrose is the shop that we are heading for,
And it feels good, when we walk through the swinging door.

We walk up and down their aisles helping ourselves,
Bewildered by the choice we have on the shelves.

If I bump into anyone, I find they are doing the same as me,
Looking for the ticket that says "Buy one and get one free."

I am always aware of a nice sound in the air,
The sound of people being polite, showing they care.

There is always a nice warm smile from the person on the till,
If you need them to help you, you know they will.

Walking back home, Wally may give a little squeak, but it's allowed,
For you do a good job Wally, and of you I am proud.

Wally the Trolley will wait in the hall again, until I am ready,
Because he knows that he keeps me upright and steady.

₋nd of Silence

I was on holiday, and everything was going great,
I was here at Pontins, with Hilda my mate.

And just when we were really going to town,
My precious hearing aid broke, and let me down.

Suddenly gone were all the sounds loud enough to wake the dead,
In their place was the awful sound that I most dread,

It was the sound of silence, making it hard to communicate,
Leaving me feeling stupid and in a nervous state.

Bang went my confidence, and any joy I had,
I thought about my friend and it made me feel bad.

But I managed to smile and muddle through,
Thanking Hilda for her help, that's the least I could do.

It sounds so dramatic; I don't mean it to be,
I just like writing things that happen, down on paper you see.

Enough of my moaning, I must not turn into a cynic,
So I am off to see my friends at the hearing clinic.

They are kind and understanding it wont take them long,
To put things right, whatever has gone wrong.

What would deaf people do without you, however would we live?
My grateful thanks to all of you, for all the help you give.

Woodley Wilkins

When I go shopping on my own,
I feel anxious, nervous and so alone.

You see, I would like someone to be with me,
But that is not possible, it can't always be.

So I have invented a walking friend, someone to be my guide,
Together we will go shopping, walking side by side.

A sort of Harry Potter if you know what I mean,
Someone who is always with me although he can't be seen.

I have to give a name for my imaginary friend,
The list of names I have, just goes on without end.

But the name Woodley Wilkins springs to mind,
It conjures up a person, not wise but kind.

Woodley Wilkins is also known as Self Confidence so now you can see,
Why I need to take Woodley Wilkins along with me.

If he can stay with me for the journey there and back,
I will be all right, because self-confidence is the thing I lack.

And if I hang on to Wally the Trolley I wont need my white stick,
And together we can face the on-coming traffic.

When we return a sense of achievement is what I will feel,
But I say to myself "Woman get real."

A walk down the road is all you have done,
You have not climbed Mount Everest or been in a Marathon Run.

But that wont stop me punching the air,
As Woodley Wilkins and I flop into a chair.

Life in the Old Girl Yet

I have wrote a lot of verses over the years,
Some have produced smiles, others a few tears.

I am not sure what this one will do,
It's a theme that to me is completely new.

This verse is about my disabilities, and it goes a bit against the grain,
Because other people have disabilities and they don't complain.

I try not to feel sorry for myself, which is easier said than done,
For being registered deaf and nearly blind isn't exactly a barrel of fun.

But Catherine Court is full of lovely people, who try to understand,
And they are always available to give a helping hand.

Not just for me, for anyone in need,
Are they good Samaritans? Oh yes indeed.

When I started this verse I was very much in doubt,
I didn't have a clue what it would be about.

But now I know, it was to give me something to do,
And it gave me a good feeling to be writing to all of you.

What good therapy this is turning out to be,
I thought I couldn't write... but I can you see.

It was lovely Brian's suggestion, I have him to thank for this,
Next time I see him I'll reward him with a kiss.

I was feeling as miserable as sin earlier on,
Now thankfully that feeling has nearly all gone.

And I am looking forward to writing my next verse you bet,
There's still life in the old girl yet.

Thank you for reading my book of verses. I have derived much pleasure in writing them and hope that you too have enjoyed sharing part of my life.

God Bless.

Eileen.